"Original and hilarious." —*School Library Journal*

"Highly amusing new series starter. . . . Skye gives Rob a self-deprecating charm and highlights the pleasures of books both subtly and effectively." —*Booklist*

"This pitch-perfect offering should appeal to reluctant readers, not to mention the legion of Wimpy Kid fans." —*Shelf Awareness*

"Skye captures all the silly action in the winning text-plus-cartoons format. . . ." —*Publishers Weekly*

"The text is hysterical by itself, but acts as the straight man in relation to the one-two punch of the childlike drawings and captions. . . . Get multiple copies of this book: it will fly off the shelves." —*School Library Journal*

KATFISH

THE CREATURE
FROM MY
CLOSET

OBERT SKYE

SQUARE
FISH

Christy Ottaviano Books

Henry Holt and Company ✦ New York

SQUARE
FISH

An imprint of Macmillan Publishing Group, LLC
175 Fifth Avenue, New York, NY 10010
mackids.com

Square Fish and the Square Fish logo are trademarks of Macmillan and
are used by Henry Holt and Company under license from Macmillan.

Our books may be purchased in bulk for promotional, educational, or business use. Please contact
your local bookseller or the Macmillan Corporate and Premium Sales Department at (800)
221-7945 ext. 5442 or by e-mail at MacmillanSpecialMarkets@macmillan.com.

Library of Congress Cataloging-in-Publication Data
Skye, Obert.
Katfish / Obert Skye.
pages   cm — (The creature from my closet ; 4)
Summary: Principal Smelt has created the Fun-ger Games for Softrock Middle School's
students, and Rob Burnside, his life in ruins, hopes that Katfish, a cross between Katniss
and the Little Mermaid created in Rob's closet, will help with game tips, advice about girls,
and how to get people to stop hating him.
ISBN 978-1-250-14367-9 (paperback)   ISBN 978-1-62779-247-9 (ebook)
[1. Middle schools—Fiction. 2. Schools—Fiction. 3. Interpersonal relations—Fiction.
4. Family life—Fiction. 5. Monsters—Fiction. 6. Humorous stories.] I. Title.
PZ7.S62877Kat 2014   [Fic]—dc23   2014017003

Originally published in the United States by Christy Ottaviano Books/Henry Holt and Company
First Square Fish edition, 2018
Book designed by Véronique Lefèvre Sweet
Square Fish logo designed by Filomena Tuosto

1   3   5   7   9   10   8   6   4   2

AR: 4.7 / LEXILE: 700L

For my mom,
who was an *excellent* napper
and a fantastic mother

CONTENTS

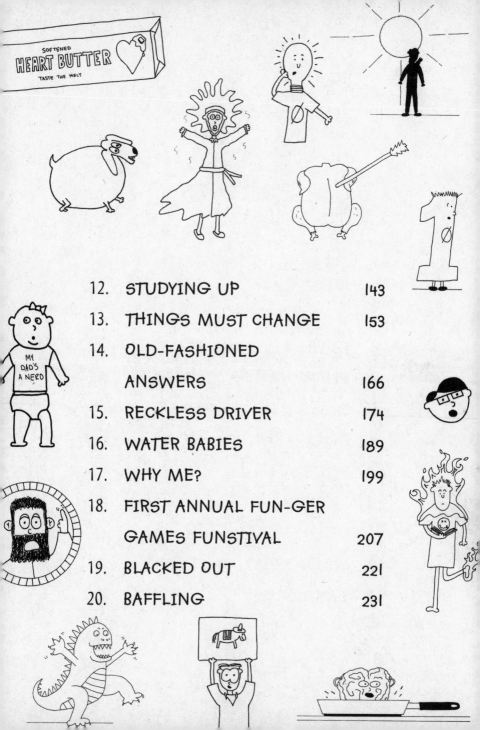

CHAPTER 1

MESS

I know, I know—I blew it. Seriously, my life has become the kind of sticky mess that other sticky messes probably gross out about.

Most of the people in my life won't even talk to me at the moment or acknowledge that I exist.

Sadly, being so disliked doesn't mean I can stop writing down or doodling what I'm going through. I would love to be buried by a big pile of leaves or blankets and left alone for the rest of my life, but there are things I have to do.

I used to have no interest in books, and I definitely had no desire to write or draw things from my life for scientific purposes. But the world needs to know about my closet and what it can do. So despite being disliked by almost everyone I know at the moment, I must keep writing.

My life is in ruins. I've let my parents down.

My older sister, Libby, hates me just as much as ever.

Janae, the girl I've been crushing on for years, won't even look at me. I could change my style completely and she still wouldn't glance my way.

Even my little brother, Tuffin, doesn't look up to me anymore.

Yes, things are uncomfortable. It feels like the time my dad did the laundry and accidentally shrunk all my clothes.

The worst part is that there's nobody to blame but me. I made this mess by lying to all of them about a lot of things. I told them that our school dance was going to be televised and that they were all going to be filmed. I told them they were going to be famous, but in the end, they were just embarrassed. I let everyone down and ruined our first school dance. Principal Smelt gave me detention for fooling everyone.

I don't think there's a single teacher or student at Softrock Middle School who isn't upset with me. Even the school announcements are painful.

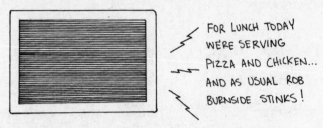

FOR LUNCH TODAY
WE'RE SERVING
PIZZA AND CHICKEN...
AND AS USUAL ROB
BURNSIDE STINKS!

One of the hipster kids at my school even

suggested that we change the pledge.

...AND TO THE ROB BURNSIDE,
WHO RUINED EVERYTHING,
ONE BIG DISAPPOINTMENT...

DOOFISTER

I wanted to explain to everyone that Pinocula had

been the cause of most of the trouble. But the

things that came out of my closet weren't really

public knowledge, and even if I wanted to spill the

beans, Pinocula had returned to the closet and I had

no proof of what had gone down.

In an effort to shame me even further, my mom threw an apology party so people could come to our house and I could publicly say I'm sorry. It was a horrible idea. Luckily only one person came—and it wasn't even someone I needed to apologize to. It was just Rex, the homeschooled boy who lived two streets over. He'd heard from someone that there was a party, so he showed up.

He thought it was a birthday party and gave me a gift. I was excited until I opened it.

Rex's mom taught yoga and was big-time into nature stuff. Last summer when Tuffin and I had been playing out in the front yard, she came over and insisted we put on a bunch of homemade sunscreen she had made in her kitchen. I didn't want to, but she stood there until we spread it all on.

It was super sticky and smelled like eggs. We could barely move once it was on. As soon as she left, Tuffin and I ran back and jumped in our swimming pool to wash it off. We splashed and swished, but it didn't come off easily and it made the surface of the pool all oily and yellow. Which was pretty embarrassing when Janae's older sister looked over the fence to see what all the splashing was about.

If you want to know the truth, I blame my closet for most of the mess I'm in. It used to be just a nice, normal walk-in closet without a door.

When I was a kid I wanted to have a science lab in it, but the only things my mom would let me experiment with were ketchup and mustard and old supplies around the house. All ketchup and cleaning supplies could really make was a mess. So I began to use my closet as a place to hide all the books my mom tried to make me read.

In time my closet became a big, sticky, booky mess. It might have remained that way forever if it hadn't been for my dad. I like my dad most of the time. He always wears a suit and a tie, and he's always super happy. He sells playground equipment for a living and loves his job. He also loves garage sales, and a while back, he found an odd door at a garage sale and brought it home. He put it on my closet, where it fit perfectly.

At first I didn't like the closet door. It was old and unusual. It had a dumb sticker on it that I couldn't get off. It was super heavy and hard to open. But the worst thing about the door had to be the doorknob. It was brass and on the knob there was a face of a little bearded man I decided to call Beardy.

Sometimes Beardy's eyes seem to wink at me, or he changes his expression to show he's disappointed.

I don't know exactly what happens behind my closet door when Beardy locks up, but my theory is that the old ketchup and cleaning supplies drip through the *books* and bring mixed-up things to life. Wonk was the first to visit, followed by Hairy, then Pinocula. And I'm pretty certain that my closet will produce something new soon, seeing how Beardy has remained locked tight for days. My hope is that it's some character big and amazing enough to help me frighten my enemies just a little.

I know it's weird to feel this way, considering all the trouble they caused, but I miss Wonk and Hairy and Pinocula. Their personalities and stories have made my life much more interesting. But now they've gone. The only reminder I have of them is the three things they've left behind. Three things that might just help me someday.

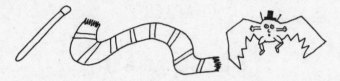

I keep Wonk's cane and Hairy's scarf on top of my dresser. As for the bat/cricket that stayed behind after Pinocula left, I have no idea where he is right now. I'm also not sure how these things they left behind will ever help me. It'd be nice to think that wherever Wonk, Hairy, and Pinocula are, maybe they're working on an idea to make my life clearer.

DO YOU HAVE ANY IDEA WHAT WE CAN DO TO HELP ROB?

HE SEEMS TO NEED A LOT OF HELP.

I COULD LIE TO SOMEONE.

CHAPTER 2

GUESS AGAIN

Friday morning I woke up happy. Not because everyone was nice to me again, but because we didn't have school. I guess the teachers were having meetings about stuff they didn't want the students to know.

I don't care what they talk about as long as it means I get to stay home. I wanted to go hang out with my friends, but as usual my mom had other plans for me.

I tried to tell my mom how important friendship is to kids, but she wasn't buying it. She gave me a list of things that she thought would help me feel better about the lies I recently told.

- FEED THE PETS
- VACUUM OUT THE CARS
- CLEAN DIRT RING IN BATHTUB
- HELP TUFFIN CLEAN THE TRASH PILE IN HIS ROOM
- TAKE BOOKS TO AUNT BETTY

The one task on the list I didn't mind doing was the first item. Our fat dog, Puck, and my uncaged, pooping bird, Fred, were the only living things in my house that were nice to me. Puck spent more time in my room, and Fred hadn't pooped on anything of mine in days. Neither of them seemed the least bit upset.

The last item on my list of chores was to take a few books over to Aunt Betty's house. Aunt Betty is really rich, but for some reason she's always borrowing books from my mom instead of buying them herself.

My sister says it's because she spends all her money on important things—like fake hair and nails. I usually don't mind if my aunt borrows stuff because both she and my mom have weird taste in books, but this time my mom was lending her one I cared about.

CLEAN SHEETS, KITTEN BURPS,
AND OTHER LITTLE JOYS OF LIFE

BY DR. MARY MARGARET MAY

THE TICKLE DIET
TICKLE YOUR WAY TO GOOD HEALTH

THIS DIET'S GOING TO GET YOU!

BY TIMMY TICKLE

MOCKINGJAY

SUZANNE COLLINS

I didn't necessarily care about clean sheets or tickling, but I did have some interest in the Hunger Games books. After I saw the first movie, everyone kept insisting there were tons of other cool things in the book that had been left out of the film. So last week without being forced, I read book one.

Now I had started book two, but my mom was letting Aunt Betty read the final book in the series. My aunt was kind of a slow reader, and I knew that when I needed it she probably wouldn't be done. Which meant I would have to wait, and waiting was not something I usually enjoyed. To me waiting was worse than having to eat something really disgusting.

I put the books in an old grocery bag and left my house. I wanted to walk with better company than just myself, so I ran across the street to Trevor's to see if he was home. Nobody at my school wanted anything to do with me, but my five friends—Teddy, Aaron, Rourk, Jack, and Trevor—hadn't completely turned their backs on me.

Trevor is my best friend. His glasses are always crooked and he's too glass-half-full sometimes, but he's my favorite person to hang out with. He's an only child and way into books and movies. He's dorky, but he doesn't do some of the dumb things my other friends do.

When I got to his house, Trevor was out front helping his mom wash her car. He wasn't allowed to come with me to my aunt's house until he was finished, so I decided to help.

It wasn't that bad a job until Trevor's mom told me that the rags we were using were actually cut-up pairs of old underwear Trevor's dad used to wear.

I didn't want anything to do with cleaning things with anyone's skivvies, so I operated the hose for a while. After the third time of accidentally squirting Trevor's mom, she excused us so we could go to my aunt's house.

Thankfully, Trevor changed his car-washing clothes. We then cut through the alleys and over into the far neighborhood back by the empty church and the Mexican restaurant with the plastic burro on the roof. Trevor was taking Spanish in school and had recently become interested in Spanish culture.

DID YOU KNOW THAT MEXICAN FOOD IS THE NUMBER TWO MOST POPULAR FOOD IN AMERICA?

* THE MOST POPULAR IS AMERICAN. USA! USA!

I said yes just so he'd stop talking. We crossed the busy road and worked our way through the unknown alleys by the dog park. While walking through the park, I thought I saw something following us. Every time I turned around, however, nobody was there.

HEY! WHAT ARE YOU LOOKING AT? THERE'S NOBODY HERE.

It seemed like I was still a bit unsettled from having used someone's old underwear. On the other side of the dog park, there was a golf course, and next to the golf course was the gated community where my aunt lived.

Who knows why some neighborhoods are gated and some aren't. If I had to guess I'd say that someone somewhere felt like they lived too close to Jack and Rourk to not have some sort of protection around their houses. My aunt had given me the code for the gate, so I punched it into the panel and we entered the neighborhood.

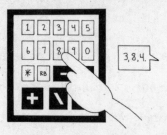

I liked Posh Peaks. I don't know why it was called this, seeing how there were no peaks. I wasn't sure what posh meant, but as usual Trevor knew.

POSH MEANS BETTER THAN OTHERS. IN SPANISH THE WORD IS "ELEGANTE."

The houses in Posh Peaks were big and old. They had tons of trees and fancy little waterfalls and streams in their front yards. Trevor and I talked about my situation as we walked. I asked him if everyone at school was still angry with me, and he said,

YES.

I asked him if Janae had said anything about me, and he said,

I asked him if it was something good, and he said,

I felt horrible about Janae. I had lied to her about the dance and had tricked her into going with me. Then to make things even stickier, she had kissed me on the cheek right before I confessed to all my lies. I felt pretty certain she would never talk to me again.

Trevor was almost as confusing as girls. My aunt's house was located at the far end of the Posh Peaks neighborhood. It was big and fat and looked like it had eaten a couple of other houses to get so huge. We walked up a stone path to a large front door. The doorbell had a little golden angel on it.

I think Beardy would love the doorbell. I pressed the button, and it chimed loudly. Before the ringing stopped, my aunt answered the door in workout clothes and holding a large cup. It was really the only way I had ever seen her look. It seemed like she was always working out and drinking water.

GOTTA STAY HYDRATED. WHOOO!

I gave her the *books*, and she invited us in for a glass of water. As we walked into the house I thought I saw something behind one of the bushes in my aunt's front yard.

After we had two huge glasses of water, we left my aunt's house and began the walk home. I kept looking around to see if maybe Jack or Teddy had followed us, but there was no sign of anyone.

So Teddy was out, but something was following us.
I felt uneasy. It reminded me of my Thumb Buddies.
Thumb Buddies were small, decorated thumbtacks
that used to be sold to kids. They stopped selling
new ones years ago due to the fact that too many
kids got poked and stabbed by them. You could still
find them at Thumb Buddies conventions or online,
but no stores sell them. My friends don't know, but
I still collect them. Three days ago I found one of
the rarest Thumb Buddies on eBay.

FAMOUS-MOVIE-STAB

It was quite a find. My Thumb Buddies didn't make me feel uneasy, but the Thumb Buddies board game did. I didn't like how bad I felt whenever I picked a bad Pin Pal card.

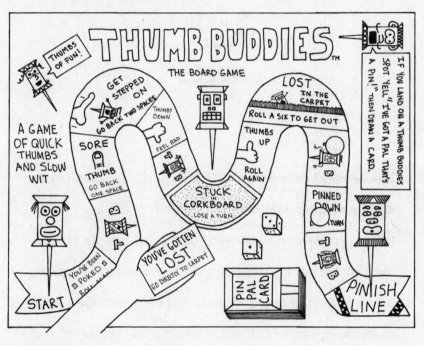

I hated to be sent to the carpet. I also hated the feeling of someone following me and Trevor.

CHAPTER 3

HOLES

Trevor and I stopped at the dog park. I couldn't hear anyone following us anymore, and Trevor's feet hurt. It was surprising how much dog poop people hadn't cleaned up. I'm not sure why, but we decided to pick up a couple long sticks and start flinging unscooped poop at trees. It was sort of like a really gross version of golf.

FORE!

A woman with an odd-looking dog thought we were trying to clean the park and actually thanked us.

After she left we started flinging poop toward the road. I thought we were being really helpful, but an old man yelled at us, so we decided to stop.

The water I had at my aunt's house made my bladder dance. So I did the brave thing and decided to use the Porta-Potty at the park.

There is nothing worse than the inside of a Porta-Potty. It smells, it's hot, and I always get light-headed.

While I was inside, Trevor started knocking on the door. I yelled for him to stop, but he knocked again. I finished and busted out. But Trevor wasn't anywhere. When I yelled his name he came out from behind a tree.

I thanked Trevor for being weird and asked him if he had seen who knocked. He told me that not only was he hiding but he had plugged his ears and shut his eyes. Apparently, he had a really difficult time being near a Porta-Potty.

After walking back through the dog park, I thought I heard someone behind us again. I turned quickly and saw someone duck behind a Dumpster. This time Trevor saw it, too.

Since there was no answer, we crept up to the Dumpster and slowly looked behind it. Nobody was there. We turned and kept walking in the direction of our homes, but about ten feet later we heard the bushes behind us shake. We spun around and saw a shadow again.

SOMEONE'S REALLY AFTER US!

FOLLOW ME. I HAVE AN IDEA.

I started to run and explain my plan. Next to my house there's a vacant lot. Someone was going to build a house there years ago but didn't, so now the lot just sits there empty. Most people think it's an eyesore, but I think it increases the value of our neighborhood. We always build dirt bike ramps or dig holes in that lot. Over the last few months, we've dug one of our best holes ever. It's about three feet wide and extremely deep. I hadn't actually measured how deep, but I wouldn't be surprised to hear someone speaking Chinese at the bottom of it.

*TRANSLATION: ANYONE UP THERE?

Two days ago after school, Jack and I covered the hole with palm leaves to make a trap. We were hoping to catch Aaron or Rourk, but so far nobody had fallen in. Now I could just lead whoever was following us to our trap. It would be just like when Wonk had fallen into a hole, only this time it would be on purpose.

Trevor and I ran past the Mexican restaurant and crossed the *busy street*. As we huffed down the alley I could hear footsteps behind us in the distance. I couldn't *see* anyone, but someone was definitely after us.

We shot out of the alley and across the street to the vacant lot. I could *see* the shadow behind us now.

I jumped over the palm leaves with Trevor. The shadow behind us fell right into our trap. Leaves snapped and crackled as whoever was after us fell into my snare. I stopped running and turned. I was thinking of celebrating how smart I was, but what I saw stopped me.

UM...IS THIS SUPPOSED TO BE A TRAP?

The first surprise was that the hole wasn't quite as deep as I thought. The second was that it wasn't Teddy or Jack chasing us. It was a girl. Trevor instantly took a small plastic comb out of his pocket and *began* to comb his hair. For some reason, I licked my palms and began slicking my hair back.

Middle school is weird for a lot of reasons, and a bunch of those reasons have to do with girls. Even my friends are affected by it. Teddy used to brag about never showering. Now he showers constantly and wears cologne. Rourk used to fart and burp in front of everyone. Now he actually tries to clench and keep his mouth closed when girls are around.

Aaron still has a hard time telling the truth, but in front of girls his lies are extra wack.

I'VE ONLY GOT 1% BODY FAT.

I CAN LIFT OVER FIVE HUNDRED POUNDS.

I'VE WON AWARDS FOR MY KISSING.

I'VE DATED HUNDREDS OF MODELS.

And Jack used to eat bugs, but now he's always worried about his breath.

I'd like to think that I wasn't quite as girl crazy, but I had done some really dumb things in the last few months and all because I wanted Janae to like me. Now, standing here in the hole we had dug was a girl I had never seen. I wanted to ask who she was, but my brain was missing a few pieces.

CHAPTER 4

BLOCK HEAD

It's not easy for a boy to describe a girl without sounding dumb, but I'm going to try. This girl had two legs and a couple of arms. Her hair was long and darkish and braided to one side. She had a body, and her face was arranged in such a way that I didn't hate looking at it. Like I said, it's not easy to describe without sounding dumb. Oh yeah, she was also wearing clothes and shoes. I had never seen her before, and the clothes she was wearing looked too heavy for the warm weather we had in

Temon. I was surprised to see her, but I was even more surprised to hear what she had to say.

HI, ROB.

Trevor looked at me and put his comb away.

YOU KNOW HER?

As I shook my head, the girl began to laugh. It wasn't the kind of laugh that made you think you'd said something funny. It was more like the kind of laugh that made you feel slightly stupid.

My jaw dropped and my heart stopped.

I rubbed my eyes and smacked my right palm against my right ear to bang the water out of it. I took a deep breath and spoke.

I was going to tell Trevor what I had figured out, but I was interrupted by my mom yelling from our front porch.

In case you don't know, my mom calls me Ribert. I'm not totally sure why, but I think it has something to do with her wanting to embarrass me as much as she can.

She didn't sound happy or mad. She was probably just making sure I came home rather than hanging out on the island in the cul-de-sac that sat in the middle of our neighborhood.

THE NEIGHBORHOOD + SPOTS OF INTEREST

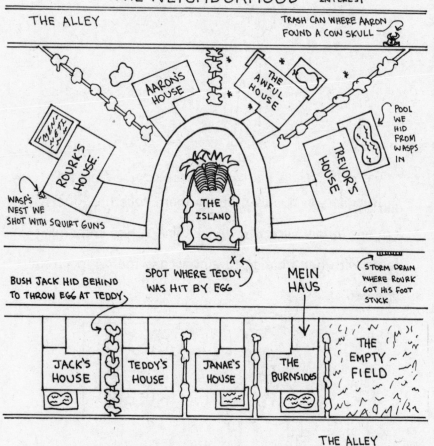

THE ALLEY

TRASH CAN WHERE AARON FOUND A COW SKULL

AARON'S HOUSE

THE AWFUL HOUSE

POOL WE HID FROM WASPS IN

ROURK'S HOUSE

TREVOR'S HOUSE

WASP'S NEST WE SHOT WITH SQUIRT GUNS

THE ISLAND

BUSH JACK HID BEHIND TO THROW EGG AT TEDDY

SPOT WHERE TEDDY WAS HIT BY EGG

MEIN HAUS

STORM DRAIN WHERE ROURK GOT HIS FOOT STUCK

JACK'S HOUSE

TEDDY'S HOUSE

JANAE'S HOUSE

THE BURNSIDES

THE EMPTY FIELD

THE ALLEY

I turned to say something to the new girl, but she had already taken off, running in the other direction. Trevor looked at me as if wanting answers. I hadn't actually seen her come from my closet, but I knew she had. I also knew I needed to talk to her.

Trevor took out his comb again, combed his hair, and then took off. I ran to my house where my mom was standing on the porch with my sister, Libby. My mom had a phone in her hand. It was bright outside, and I could see that she had a slight smile on her face. She reached out to hand me the phone.

I nervously took the phone from my mom. The voice on the other end belonged to Principal Smelt. He was way too excited for my comfort. He kept talking about how a boy like me, who everyone was mad at, just needed a push in the right direction. I could tell something dreadful was coming.

Principal Smelt's idea dealt with his music group. As most people in my neighborhood know, Principal Smelt has a two-man band called Leftover Angst. It's just him and another teacher, and they sing horrible songs about things that shouldn't be sung about.

Their singing was embarrassing, but it was even worse because Principal Smelt played the pan flute and the other teacher played the tambourine. They performed at most school functions and gatherings in our area. Last week they had played at the supermarket for Fruit Awareness Week.

Principal Smelt wanted me to play with his band at the costume festival my school was having in three days, on Monday. Of course Principal Smelt wasn't calling it a festival, he was calling it a

FUN-STIVAL!!

According to Principal Smelt, fun + festival = funstival. It was going to be like the normal fall festival where everyone wears costumes, and there would be a dunk tank and party games. But this year was going to be a little different. Principal Smelt had recently read the Hunger Games trilogy. He was so excited about it that we were going to have our own kind of Hunger Games at the funstival. Instead of calling the contest Hunger Games, he was calling it . . .

FUN-GER GAMES!

It was three days away, and I was going to have to be a part of the music. My life was bruised at the moment, and I guess he wanted to make things worse by forcing me to stand in front of everyone and play in his band. When I tried to explain to him that I had no talent, he said,

THAT'S OKAY. YOU'LL BE PLAYING THE WOOD BLOCK.

Normally even my mom wouldn't make me do something so humiliating and painful, but she was still upset about all the lies and trouble I had recently caused. She was dead set on me learning my lesson.

I hung up the phone, wishing I could die. My school already hated me, and now I would be playing the wood block at the funstival. Everyone would make fun of me. I was upset about the band, but I was also worried about what had just happened with Trevor. I needed to check my closet and then find the girl who had just run off. I quickly thought of an excuse to leave. I turned and looked at my mom.

My mom was leery at first, but when I explained that I just wanted to practice my wood blocking, she said there were some old pieces of lumber in the garage. I thanked her like I meant it and took off. I found a small piece of wood and something to hit it with. I then headed quickly to my room—I had a doorknob to question.

CHAPTER 5

DISLIKE OF COOTIES

When I got to my room, my closet door was opened a few inches and Beardy was smiling at me. I jumped toward him just as the door slammed shut. I tried as hard as I could to pry it open.

COME ON!

I knew it was useless to keep trying, but I couldn't think of what else to do. Beardy never opened up unless he wanted to. Puck barked loudly at the door as if it would help.

Libby came into my room and politely told me to shut up. When I explained to her that it was Puck barking, not me, she said,

Libby sniffed a couple of times and left. Puck growled at the closet door a few more seconds and then rolled away to find something to eat. I picked up my piece of wood as Trevor popped up at my window.

Trevor opened the window and spilled into my room. He was going on about how the girl had gotten away, but he stopped talking when he noticed the block of wood I was holding.

Trevor was really excited. He had always wanted to be in a band. His uncle had just sent him a guiro, which was a Spanish instrument made from a dried vegetable gourd that you rubbed with a stick. Trevor was always itching to play it.

So far nobody had taken Trevor up on his offer. He begged me to ask Principal Smelt if he could play at the funstival with us. When I told him we had more important things to talk about, he looked hurt.

Trevor wouldn't drop it. He made me call Principal Smelt and ask if he could play in the band with us at the funstival. He wouldn't answer my questions about the girl unless I did. So I called Principal Smelt. Not surprisingly, our principal was okay with it.

FANTASTIC! THE GUIRO IS SUCH A HAUNTING INSTRUMENT.

As soon as I hung up I asked Trevor about the girl that had *stalked* us. He got his comb out of his pocket and began to *comb* his hair again.

SHE'S NOT HERE, YOU KNOW.

IS SHE IN THE CLOSET?

NO.

I WONDER IF SHE LIKES ME.

SHE DOESN'T.

Trevor started to argue with me about how his mother thought he was handsome and how any girl would be lucky to be friends with him. I begged him to stop.

PLEASE JUST TELL ME WHAT HAPPENED TO THE GIRL.

Trevor told me that she had run past the island and slipped into the alley behind Aaron's house. He said she was a fast runner and that she didn't look very mixed-up like the other creatures who had come out of my closet in the past.

SHE'S ALL WOMAN!

PLEASE STOP TALKING.

I paced my bedroom trying to think of what to do. One piece of me wanted to go after her. Another piece was a little scared that a girl had come from my closet. Another was trying to figure out who she was, and another piece just wanted to jump into my bed and pretend my life was as normal as it used to be.

It was one thing for Wonk and Hairy and Pinocula to mess up my life, but it was something altogether different to have the visitor be a girl. Plus, she wasn't little like the others. She was relatively normal sized and wouldn't fit in my drawers or locker or backpack.

IT SMELLS LIKE FEET IN HERE.

Trevor and I crawled out my window and walked to the rock island. I scanned the area, hoping she might have come back, but there was no sign of her. Jack, Aaron, and Teddy were on the island, beneath the palm trees, carving bars of soap with kitchen knives. Jack had seen someone carving soap in a movie, and now he spent a good part of his time trying to make things. The best thing he had

ever carved was a bird's nest with three eggs. His
other attempts were awful.

DOG   PUMPKIN   BIRD'S NEST

Aaron was apparently bored with carving; he
chucked his piece of soap at me and hit me in my
knees. I picked it up and threw it back at him. Jack
was suddenly the soap police.

CAREFUL, SOAP'S NOT CHEAP.

Jack wanted us to sit down and carve our own creations, but first we needed to find the new guest. I told them all that we were looking for something, and they became very curious. I knew they'd find out sooner or later, so I decided to spill the beans. I told them about the girl who had followed us, and how I thought she must have come from my closet, and how we now had to find her.

They all jumped up and volunteered to help. When they asked what she looked like I finally said what I had been thinking since I first saw her.

I thought Aaron and Jack didn't care for *The Hunger Games*, but they seemed pretty pumped up about Katniss.

NOT THAT I KNOW HER NAME. I JUST REMEMBER THAT IT RHYMED WITH FATNESS.

For those of you who don't know, *The Hunger Games* is all about a dark future where the world's gone nuts and kids have to compete against each other for food. It's a cool story, but it's not always happy. Katniss is a strong, brave girl who volunteers to take her little sister's place in the games. She does a bunch of amazing girl-power things, and she has mad bow and arrow skills. There are a couple of boys in the book that like her and a few grown-ups that don't. In the end she . . . well . . . I don't want to spoil the ending.

Trevor started to say something about how
important it was to look for her before the trail grew
cold, but he was stopped by Teddy who suddenly
looked scared and was pointing to the top of the
palm trees above us. I glanced up. But because of
the sun I couldn't see anything besides the shadow
of the huge leaves.

I should have looked harder.

CHAPTER 6

BANG A GONG

I glanced back down and saw Aaron pointing. I turned my head up, and as I did, something came flying down toward us from the palm leaves. It hit Rourk hard and slammed him against the ground. I fell backward as Rourk tried to push whatever it was off him. Dirt flew up and got into my eyes as the sound of Rourk struggling filled my ears. I wiped my eyes, and there she was. She had Rourk's arms pinned behind his back as he was pressed belly-first against the ground. Rourk was kicking

and screaming, but it wasn't doing him any good.
She pulled up on his arms as he lay on the ground.

I wondered if Rourk even knew what his quads were
and if I should try to help. I didn't know what to do.
I looked at my other friends, but they were all just
standing there. That's not completely true—Trevor
and Teddy had taken their combs out and were
fixing their hair.

The girl let go of Rourk's arms and rolled him over onto his back. She pinned down both of his arms and stared directly into his eyes.

The girl jumped off Rourk. She tried to stare into Aaron's eyes.

A noisy truck was coming down the road, and the tree-climbing girl glanced at it. Rourk stood up, trying

to look cool about being knocked down by a tree girl.
I was going to say something, but she spoke first.

Before I could ask her what the heck she was
talking about, she turned and took off running. She
darted in front of the oncoming truck and off through
a distant alley before I could tell my legs to run.

My friends had a lot of questions for me. Most of them had to do with whether or not I thought the new girl liked them.

I couldn't really blame them. There was something about her that made me want to stand up straight and make sure my socks were clean.

Of all the questions my friends were asking, Trevor's was the most interesting.

WHAT DO YOU THINK SHE MEANT BY "TWO DOWN"?

I was going to admit that I had no idea, when an odd noise sounded. I should tell you that the noise was not one that we heard often in our neighborhood.

Six houses down, there lives a man named Mr. Foote. In his backyard he has a huge gong that he rings only twice a year—once on Chinese New Year and once on his wedding anniversary. It's an important gong, and when he does ring it, it's so loud that the whole neighborhood can hear it. A year ago Jack mistakenly hopped over Mr. Foote's fence and accidentally rang the gong.

Mr. Foote was usually pretty nice, but he was not
happy about that. He threatened to take Jack to
court and sue his parents. Apparently, the gong
means a lot to him, and now it had just gone off—
twice! We knew it wasn't Chinese New Year, and Mr.
Foote's anniversary was in the summer. Jack wasn't
about to take the blame.

Mr. Foote came running out of his house. He spotted us all on the island and jumped up and down as he ran toward us. I thought about running myself, but he had to know that with us standing on the island, there was no way we could have rung the gong. He yelled at us as we all stood there speechless and with blank faces.

Then he stormed off, promising to find out who had done it. Even though Mr. Foote was six houses down we could hear the sound of him slamming his door as he went back into his house. I looked at my friends. Trevor whispered,

I nodded. I was 99 percent sure that it had been the tree girl who had rung the gong. There was only a tiny bit of me that felt differently.

The girl had taken off in the direction of Mr. Foote's house, and she seemed like the kind of person who would gong someone's gong when she shouldn't.

Before we could figure anything out, my mom spotted me at the island and called me back home to practice my wood block. Trevor went home to practice his guiro, and the rest of my friends continued to practice their soap carving.

PONY

CHAPTER 7

ROTISSERIE CHICKEN

After I hit the *block of wood* for a while, my mom
asked me to please stop and go clean the pool. I
was able to stop hitting the block, but I couldn't
stop thinking about the girl.

Of course there was always a little bit of me that thought about pie. But at the moment I didn't know where the girl was and I didn't have any pie. I did, however, have jobs to do. Normally I don't mind taking care of the pool—I get to test the chemicals and use the net to scoop dead bugs off the top of the water. But I don't like the job when I have to watch Tuffin at the same time. He always swims as I clean, and if he's not splashing me, he's making the pool dirtier.

My dad came out to swim laps, but when he saw Tuffin was swimming, he decided to do something else.

While my dad was stretching, I saw something fly up over the alley wall behind our house and into our backyard. The object fell to the ground with a thud. Two seconds later, closet girl hopped up over the fence and landed on her feet right next to the object. My dad had his back turned doing his stretches, so he didn't see any of it. I ran over to the girl and looked down at what she had thrown over.

Apparently, she had used her bow and arrow to shoot a chicken that someone had been roasting.

My dad started to do toe touches. As he was bending over with his head upside down, he spotted me and my visitor.

My dad smiled and stood up straight. My father rarely looked mad. In fact, most of the time he was smiling. Now, as he spotted me talking to a strange girl in our backyard, he looked even happier than usual. He spun around and raced over to us. I was scared he was going to knock us both down since he was walking so fast. He skidded to a halt in front of us and stuck out his hand.

HOW DO YOU DO?

I had no idea how she would act toward my father, or how she would answer his question. I knew I needed to speak up. I needed to think of something quick. My brain ran around inside my head trying to figure out what to say and do.

I had *been* trying really hard not to lie lately. Pinocula had made things uncomfortable with all the lies and confusion he had put me through. I figured it was best to stick as close to the truth as possible.

It wasn't a real lie, but it was definitely a stretch of the truth. Despite what Beardy might say, there really is no Closet family. And since she looked, and acted, strong and independent like Katniss, I figured Kat would do as a nickname. My dad noticed what was lying on the ground and leaned in to ask me something. I didn't really have an answer so I made something up.

IS THAT A CHICKEN?

ITS A WELCOME CHICKEN. THAT'S WHAT THEY DO.

HOW FASCINATING.

Kat was cool. She smiled at my dad and acted like what I was saying made sense. The characters that came from my closet usually were willing to help me keep their purpose a secret, and Kat was no different. I was a little nervous when my dad asked her what country she was from, but she answered,

My dad smiled. I think he thought she said the country of Panama because he said,

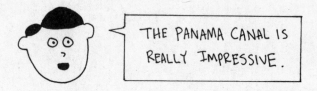

My dad kept talking. He was being his typical friendly self. He told Kat how he had seen a show on TV about the Panama Canal and how hard it was to build. He asked Kat about what kind of playground equipment they had in her country, and she told them there really wasn't any.

My father loved talking about his job, and now here was a foreigner in his backyard who had apparently grown up without slides and swings.

My father told Kat how important tire swings and sliding poles can *be* in preventing kids from becoming criminals.

My dad invited Kat to have dinner with us. I thought it was a bad idea, but there was something about Kat that made me want her around. She was strong, and interesting, and so different from the other girls I knew. It's not that she was better than Janae. It's just that she was speaking to me and Janae wasn't. Plus, Kat had to be here for a reason. Everyone who came out of my closet had taught me something. Kat was also different because I had already read the book she had come from, so I sort of felt like I knew her already. Maybe she was here because I had everything figured out and now I needed a girlfriend.

SO WILL YOU COME TO DINNER WITH ROB?

I AM SUPER HUNGRY.

FANTASTIC!

My dad told her to come at six, and Kat turned, looked up at the low sun, and licked her finger to test the wind. She then quickly jumped back over the wall and ran off down the alley.

IT'S FASCINATING HOW DIFFERENT CULTURES ARE.

I loved my dad, but sometimes he was just plain clueless. I finished cleaning the pool while my father finished his exercises. Tuffin wouldn't get out of the pool, so I was forced to use the net.

YOU'RE TOO OLD FOR THIS.

THANK YOU.

CHAPTER 8

SHARING CAN BE MESSY

I don't want you to read too much into this, but I actually took a shower and changed my clothes before dinner.

WHAT? I WAS SWEATY, AND I WANT TO MAKE SURE I DON'T SMELL WHEN KAT COMES TO DINNER.

Trevor called and I made the mistake of telling him that Kat was going to eat with us. He was so jealous, he hung up on me. I thought that would be the end of it, but ten minutes before dinner he showed up at my house, hinting that he would like to eat with us.

My mom fell for it and invited him. Apparently, Trevor had told my other friends, because one by one they showed up at my house, begging to join us for dinner.

So by the time it was dinner, all my friends were there but there was no sign of Kat. My dad had mentioned to my mother that a foreign exchange student would be joining us, so she had made a ton of food.

Right before my dad started to say a prayer and bless the meal, the doorbell rang. All my friends and I jumped up and ran to get it. There was no one at the front door.

When we got back to the table, however, Kat was sitting in a chair next to Libby.

Apparently, Kat liked to create diversions. She had rung the front doorbell and slipped in the back door. We were all shocked to see her. My dad tried to make things better by explaining how Kat's ways might be strange to us, but that different cultures did things differently.

FOR EXAMPLE, DID YOU KNOW THAT IN RUSSIA THEY NEVER POINT AT ANYTHING?

I didn't know where my dad was getting his information, but I had a feeling he was wrong. My friends and I took our seats, bummed that Kat had decided to sit between Libby and Tuffin. My dad told Kat that we usually bowed our heads and prayed before eating. We all lowered our heads, except for Jack, as my dad said an unusual prayer.

AND BLESS THAT KIDS WITHOUT A PROPER PLACE TO PLAY MIGHT FIND A KIND PLAYGROUND SALESMAN IN THEIR AREA. AND BLESS THAT OUR NEW FRIEND WILL NOT THINK OUR FOOD IS STRANGE OR DISGUSTING.

My dad didn't need to worry about that. I'd never seen anyone attack food like Kat did. If she found my mom's food to be strange, she sure didn't show it. She shoved whole rolls in her mouth and drank gravy straight from the gravy bowl. I think if any other girl, besides Janae, had done that I would have thought it was disgusting, but with Kat it wasn't so bad.

Everyone seemed to love her. My mom thought she was interesting, my dad thought she brought culture to our home, Tuffin thought she was funny, and Libby liked her style.

My friends were all trying so hard to prove they had good manners that it was beginning to get awkward. Each kept trying to act more polite than the other until they all ended up screaming at one another.

I don't think Kat was impressed. When she wasn't eating, she was busy talking to Libby. This was not a good thing. None of the creatures who had previously come from my closet had been normal size. I had kept them hidden, and for the most part, they had been my problem alone. Pinocula had tried to pass as my cousin, but other than that, they had *stayed* mostly out of sight. Not Kat. She seemed to have no problem letting everyone know she was around. I also noticed that since I had read *The Hunger Games* I knew the answers to all the questions people asked her. My dad questioned her about her parents, and for some reason I spoke up.

SHE LIVES IN DISTRICT TWELVE AND SHE HAS A LITTLE SISTER NAMED PRIMROSE. HER DAD DIED IN A MINING ACCIDENT. SHE'S A HUNTER, AND SHE SELLS HER GOODS AT THE HUB.

My mom looked at me like I was nuts. I suddenly remembered that she had read the books and would know I was talking about Katniss. I thought she was going to bust me, but she just said,

I THINK YOUR FATHER WAS ASKING KAT.

So Kat started talking. She went on about everything. Most of the stuff about her I knew. There were a few times, however, when her story didn't quite hold up to the book I had read. For example, she complained a couple of times about her feet hurting, and when my dad asked her if her mother worked, she said,

ACTUALLY, I WAS RAISED BY MY GRANDMOTHER.

I figured these were things I would have known if I had finished the second book in the Hunger Games series. In between all the questions and answers, Kat just kept on eating. She ate so much that in less than twenty minutes all the food on the table was gone. The only remaining food was on everyone else's plate.

Jack offered to give Kat what he had left, but Teddy told her that Jack had licked all the food on his plate, so she should eat his. Rourk picked up his roll and tried to hand it to Kat, but Aaron wouldn't have it. He grabbed the roll from Rourk and handed Kat a fistful of his mashed potatoes.

Now was my moment. While Libby was grossing out, I scraped my meat off my plate onto Kat's. Trevor didn't like that.

In the spirit of sharing, Trevor tossed her a handful of his peas.

The peas bounced off her dish and onto the floor. Tuffin picked up his plate and heaved it at my dad. My dad dodged the plate, which hit Jack in the back of the head. Jack wasn't mad—he now had more food to give Kat. She was just a girl, but for some reason, Kat made me and my friends act like idiots. It felt like my brain was being spun around and around and that the only way I could think straight was to get Kat to like me. My friends were also having a difficult time controlling their actions and emotions. We wanted Kat to like us so desperately that we all began throwing food at her to eat. Teddy grabbed my mom's plate, and Rourk grabbed Libby's.

My mom and Libby were shouting and trying to make us stop. My dad got up and grabbed his video camera to film the fight. By the time we all ran out of food and came to our senses, Kat was

covered in food. It was not pretty.

There was food dripping from the ceiling. There

was food on the walls, food on the floor, and food in

everyone's hair.

My dad tried to explain to Kat how this was just a cultural misunderstanding, but she was already up and heading for the back door. She stopped in front of Teddy and looked him in the eyes. Teddy seemed as if he was going to throw up from nervousness. Kat blinked and said,

Kat left through the back door while Teddy wobbled and shook. My mom looked at me and my friends.

Whenever the house was a mess, my mom would just look at us and announce that she was going to nap. I always tried to get out of the room before she could tell me to clean up while she slept, but this time I was too slow. She was going to take a nap, and my friends and I were going to have to clean up everything.

Trevor stayed, but everyone else left. Libby went off to do homework I know she didn't have. Tuffin went off to watch a movie he had already seen a thousand times. My dad went off to watch TV and think about what we had done. Trevor and I were on our own.

Trevor and I cleaned everything up, including ourselves, then went to the garage to work on our wood blocking and guiro skills. The funstival was only three days away, and we needed all the practice we could get. Even while practicing, it was hard not to think of Kat.

Down the street the sound of Mr. Foote's gong rang out. The noise filled the neighborhood and then faded. I looked at Trevor and shivered.

KAT DID SAY THREE DOWN.

She was counting down something, but I had no idea what she meant by it all. Trevor seemed excited.

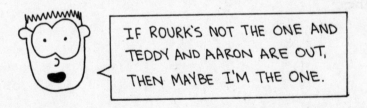

IF ROURK'S NOT THE ONE AND TEDDY AND AARON ARE OUT, THEN MAYBE I'M THE ONE.

I didn't want to be mean, but there was no way Trevor was the one—at best he was the two. Of course in my mind I had a pretty good idea who "the one" actually was.

I just hoped that being number one was a good thing.

CHAPTER 9

ONLINE

Trevor left after we practiced for about an hour. I don't think people really need to practice things like the wood block and guiro, but we stood there scraping and hitting things until we felt like we were pros.

After I got ready for bed I sat down in front of the family computer to do a little research. We had only one computer, and my parents made us keep it on a small table in the middle of our family room.

My dad tried to make it sound like it was a good thing, but Libby and I knew the real reason was because our parents wanted to know what we were doing. We used to keep the computer in the office nook near the kitchen, until Libby got busted looking up

That was when my dad decided to put the computer in the most public place in the house. I didn't really care because I usually used it only for games or homework. Tonight, however, I needed it for other reasons. I was having multiple girl problems, and I wanted to see if there was something I could do to correct them. Janae still wouldn't speak to me, and now Kat was here. I wasn't exactly smooth in the "lady" department.

I had seen a TV show where they gave out some advice to people who were having trouble with their girlfriends. They had mentioned a website where you could find ideas to help make things better.

WWW.YOU_MESSED_UP_BIG_TIME.COM

I typed in the address and pressed ENTER. There were tons of dumb ideas for boys to impress the girl of their dreams. They seemed silly, but it said they were guaranteed to work. Quickly, I wrote down a few. My dad came into the room and saw the list I was writing.

WELL, IT LOOKS LIKE MY BOY HAS GIRLS ON HIS MIND.

I just nodded and quietly hoped he would go away. My dad started talking about how he used to impress my mom. He went on and on about all the cute things he did. He described how he used to comb his hair and polish his shoes so that ...

...YOUR MOM WOULD KNOW I'M A PLAYER.

I wanted to simultaneously throw up and die, but he kept on talking. He told me about their first date, their second date, and their third date.

THE THIRD DATE WAS A LOT LIKE THE SECOND DATE, BUT INSTEAD OF BUMPER CARS THERE WAS A FERRIS WHEEL.

He told me what flowers were appropriate for a fourth date and how girls love it when you call them by their first and last names. He kept talking about my mother and his relationship with her so much that I thought maybe it would just *be* better for me to become a monk and never even date girls.

I thanked my dad for no reason and ran off with my list. When I got to my room I closed my door and there was Kat. I screamed in the most manly way I could.

Kat had come through my window, and she was trying to get back into the closet. Puck was there with her. He was obviously not a very good guard dog. Kat pulled as hard as she could on the closet doorknob. I explained to her that Beardy wouldn't open up until the time was right.

BUT I FEEL LIKE THERE'S A PART OF ME MISSING.

I knew what Kat meant. My closet usually mixed creatures up, but she didn't seem to be a mash-up. I thought maybe if we took a moment to think about why she was here it would help.

Kat told me she had been using her bow and arrows to shoot at the gong. She kept them hidden so she wouldn't waste the arrows. It wasn't easy for me to talk to girls, but I just went for it. I told Kat about everything I had learned about Katniss from reading *The Hunger Games*. Kat told me that it did sound a lot like her, but there was another part of her that didn't match up with Katniss.

Kat couldn't whistle either, which was weird, seeing how in *The Hunger Games* she could. I didn't know why she wanted to sing, but whenever she tried, nothing came out of her mouth.

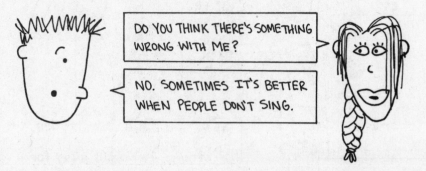

DO YOU THINK THERE'S SOMETHING WRONG WITH ME?

NO. SOMETIMES IT'S BETTER WHEN PEOPLE DON'T SING.

Kat knew she was here to help me, but she wasn't totally sure how yet. When I suggested she could start by telling Janae that I wasn't such a bad guy, she smiled and asked me if she could read my copy of *The Hunger Games*. It was a weird request, but I found my copy and gave it to her. She thanked me and promised she was going to find a way to help me, then she climbed out the window.

I closed the window behind her. Kat was something else. I mean, she was sort of interesting. I sat on my bed and looked at the list of ideas I had gotten from the internet to impress girls. I wanted to get Janae to forgive me, but for some reason every time I saw Kat, my thoughts about her got bigger while my thoughts about Janae shrunk.

I changed into one of my dad's old concert T-shirts and got ready for bed. Then I found the second book in the Hunger Games series, *Catching Fire*, and began to read.

CHAPTER 10

GOOD IDEA

Books and I have an unusual relationship. I used to
hate reading. My fourth-grade teacher, Mr. Nark, used
to say that books were like a garden, and if we didn't
pick them and "weed" them, they would die. It was
annoying because he said the whole thing in baby talk.

WE NEED TO WEED AND
WEED AND WEED BOOKS.

BABY ♡s
BOOKS

CHARLOTTE'S
WEB

I know Mr. Nark was trying to help, but it didn't. If I really had had a *book garden,* the books would have died long ago.

But now that I was in middle school, I was beginning to feel differently. I'd had a real *change of heart.*

Sure, the main reason for how I now felt about books and reading had to do with my closet. Books had come alive in my room and made life exciting. It seemed like every day there were things that books made a little bit better or more interesting. I had even gone to the library once for fun.

IT'S TIME TO GET MY BOOK ON!

I had gotten faster at reading, and I wasn't scared to start books that were more than a half-inch thick. I read a good chunk of *Catching Fire* before I went to bed, and when I woke up, I read a little more. I hopped out of bed, got dressed, and studied my list of ideas to help me win back Janae. Some of them were too stupid to even consider.

There were really only a few that I would even consider. The safest one seemed to be making a poster that I could put in Janae's front yard. The list suggested that I make it look like one of those posters that people put out on their lawn when they want other people to know who they're voting for.

So I got some markers and poster board from my mom's craft room. I then sat down on my bedroom floor and began to create. I had barely gotten the first word drawn when my friends began showing up at my window.

I HEARD SOMEONE DRAWING.

Jack had really good ears. I let him in, and two minutes later Teddy was there. He was followed by Rourk, then Aaron, and finally Trevor. It wasn't unusual for my friends to crawl through my window on a Saturday, but it was only eight in the morning and they were all showered and looked spiffed up. I told them Kat wasn't here, and they *seemed* disappointed. When I asked them to help me with my signs, they seemed even more disappointed. Luckily Trevor was still his usual positive self.

I WANNA DRAW A BURRO.

I gave Trevor a piece of poster board, and he grabbed some markers. Not wanting to be left out, my other friends took their own pieces of poster board and began to draw on them. I explained that they needed to make signs about how sorry I was and that the signs should be positive and help Janae think about forgiving me. I had lied to Janae and she had kissed me before she had found out that

I had tricked her into going to the dance. Things needed to be fixed. Everyone began to draw and create. It made me feel really good that my friends were helping. I really felt that after Janae saw the posters her heart would soften.

It was kind of stupid for me to feel good. When my friends were done, it was obvious that I had asked the wrong people to help me make posters.

I took the signs from my friends and thanked them for nothing. Jack said it was a stupid idea anyway, so I showed them the list of other dating tips.

1. POINT TO THE SKY AND TELL HER YOU'VE NAMED A STAR AFTER HER.
2. DRESS UP LIKE CUPID FOR A DAY.
3. WRITE FUN SAYINGS ON HER CAR WITH SQUIRT MUSTARD.
4. MAKE FAKE VOTING POSTERS AND PUT THEM IN HER YARD.
5. WEAR A FANCY BOW TIE AND SPEAK WITH AN ACCENT.
6. PUT ADORABLE SAYINGS INSIDE A LOT OF BALLOONS.
7. FAKE AN INJURY SO SHE'LL MAKE YOU SOUP.
8. DANCE IN FRONT OF HER.
9. MAKE CUTE ANIMAL NOISES.
10. FILL HER LOCKER WITH M&M'S.
11. GIVE UP AND LIVE A LONELY LIFE.

The only person willing to suggest one was Jack.

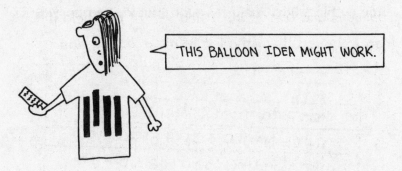

THIS BALLOON IDEA MIGHT WORK.

My mom had a big plastic container filled with hundreds of balloons in her craft room. I got them and we all wrote a bunch of cute sayings on small slips of paper. I didn't check them, but my friends promised they weren't bad.

TODAY IS A GREAT DAY TO FORGIVE ROB.

I GUESS ROB LIKES MAKING YOU MAD.

ROB MESSED UP. ARE YOU REALLY THAT SURPRISED?

ROB BURNSIDE IS NOT THAT BAD OF A GUY.

DON'T YOU THINK ROB NEEDS TO SHAPE UP?

I stuck one of the pieces of paper in one of the balloons and blew it up. I tied it shut and held it for everyone to look at.

Jack stabbed the balloon with a pencil, and a loud pop echoed around my room. We all covered our ears as the little paper drifted to the ground. It was loud, but the idea was kind of cool. I figured if we blew up fifty, stuffed them with notes, and left them in Janae's front yard she would have to forgive me. The only problem was that the noise from the popped balloon had caused my mother to come and investigate. She knocked on my bedroom door and asked,

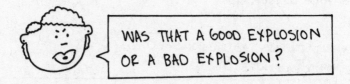

WAS THAT A GOOD EXPLOSION OR A BAD EXPLOSION?

I yelled back,

GOOD!

My mom twisted my bedroom doorknob. I sent all my friends back out the window as fast as I could and slipped the posters under the bed. I grabbed my book to make it look like I was reading. My mom came in and asked me what that good explosion had been. I blamed it on the one thing I could think of.

Puck looked guilty. My mom noticed the book I was holding and started to tell me about how much she'd enjoyed it. It was always weird to read books that my parents liked. I couldn't tell if it made me like the book more or less. My mom gave me a list of Saturday jobs I needed to do. I wasn't happy about the jobs, but I was happy that she didn't question me further about the popping balloon. I didn't think she would notice the missing supplies,

Knowing that she only went into her craft room twice a year and it was usually just to find scissors to cut a tag off something. Before she left I asked,

UM...AFTER MY JOBS COULD I JUST HANG OUT AT THE ISLAND?

My mom must have been in a good mood because she didn't say yes or no. She just turned around and walked down the hall. In my mom's language that was a yes. I did all my jobs as fast as I could. I cleaned my room, helped Tuffin clean his, emptied the dishwasher, vacuumed the family room, and gave Puck a super-quick bath.

I was going for speed, not quality. It might not have been the best thing to do, but I had other, more urgent things to get to.

CHAPTER 11

SMUDGED

As soon as my jobs were done I sprinted out the front door and over to the island. Nobody was there. I heard Trevor yelling at me from the direction of Janae's house. I couldn't see anyone, but stepping up to her house, I could hear my friends in the tree next to Janae's driveway.

WHAT ARE YOU DOING?

WAITING FOR YOU.

I climbed up in the tree and sat on the branch next to Aaron. Jack and Rourk were both holding two big garbage bags stuffed with inflated balloons. Teddy explained that they had filled the balloons with the notes and now they were waiting for Janae to come home from her tennis lessons so that they could . . .

I explained to them that the idea was to make Janae like me, not hate me more. They all looked disappointed.

They all nodded. It had been Jack's idea. He thought that the messages would have more of an impact if they were in water balloons.

My talking was interrupted by the sound of Janae's mom's car pulling into her driveway. All of us froze.

Janae got out of her car with two of her friends. Her mom, who had been driving, got out and went inside the house. Janae stood near the tree, talking loudly to her friends.

As Janae's friends talked, Rourk began to whisper about how much his butt hurt sitting in the tree. I whispered that all of him would hurt if he didn't keep quiet. Teddy sneezed, but luckily Trevor covered it up with a birdcall he had learned in Scouts. Janae and her friends looked up, but from where they were they couldn't see us. We might have gone unnoticed, but a bird flew into Aaron's big hair and began to make a nest.

UH...GUYS. I THINK I'M ABOUT TO FREAK OUT.

The bird pecked around at Aaron's head, and he let loose with a huge scream. Rourk fell from the tree, hollering and pulling Aaron down with him. Teddy shifted to avoid Aaron, and the branch beneath him snapped. All the balloons fell from the bags as Jack and Teddy pulled me and Trevor down with them. Balloons splattered everywhere as Janae and her friends screamed almost as loud as we did. Rourk rolled a good ten feet, knocking Janae's friends over like bowling pins. By the time we were all done falling, we were just a big pile of wet arms and legs. Janae was the only one still standing. She stared at me, and her mouth did that thing that is the opposite of smiling:

⌒

Janae looked at all the popped balloons and the little pieces of white paper littering the ground. I could see a few of the messages around me. They were smeared because my brilliant friends had filled the balloons with water. Janae bent down and picked up one of the notes.

ROB BURNSIDE IS ⋕⋕⋕
⋕⋕A⋕ BAD ⋕⋕ ⋕ GUY.

Janae looked at me like I was a piece of moldy meat that someone had dipped in barf and then sneezed on.

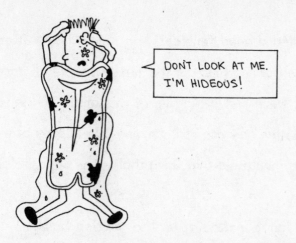

She helped her friends up as I tried to apologize.
She wasn't listening. Her friends left, and Janae
slammed the door on me and my friends as she
went inside her house.

We were all just sitting there like babies when
the shadow of someone drifted over us. I held my
hand in front of the sun to see better.

The arrows gave her away. I guess Kat was
thinking about shooting the gong soon. All my friends
were suddenly jumping up and clearing their throats.
Trevor said Kat's name, and as I got to my feet,
she grabbed him by the right elbow and gazed into
his eyes. Trevor had never looked happier.

Kat let go of a very sad-looking Trevor. She looked in my direction. I thought about saying something clever, but I had nothing clever to say. Then she took off running. I was going to chase her, but she was a much faster runner, and I had a good idea where she was going. We all watched her disappear down a far alley as we dusted ourselves off and shook water from our bodies. Trevor was pretty shook up about Kat saying he wasn't the one.

AT LEAST I STILL HAVE MY MUSIC.

Trevor began picking up the little slips of paper and bits of balloons. He was mumbling something about how he probably needed a siesta. Jack started to make fun of me for trying to impress

Janae. Remembering it was his idea to fill the balloons with water, I turned and confronted him.

WHY'D YOU PUT WATER IN THOSE?

WHY DOES ANYONE DO ANYTHING?

NOW JANAE HATES ME AND SO DOES KAT.

THEY HATED YOU BEFORE.

The gong in Mr. Foote's backyard rang out. I had been right about where Kat was going. We all looked at each other with a new sense of panic. It was one thing to have Janae and her friends mad at us. It would be even worse if Mr. Foote thought we were the ones abusing his gong. All of us took off running in separate directions to our houses. Five of us screamed in English as we ran.

CHAPTER 12

STUDYING UP

It was terrifying to wait at my house for Mr. Foote to come and accuse me of ringing his gong. I knew that at any moment the police would show up and I would be the one blamed.

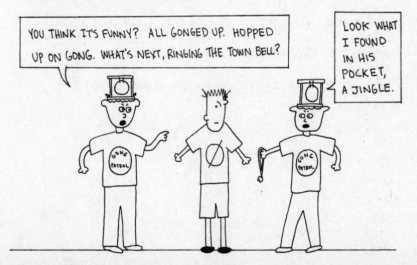

No one came. In fact, before I knew it most of Saturday had slipped away and it was late afternoon. My mom had been far less disappointed in me today, so after dinner I asked her as nicely as I could if I could hang out with my friends.

Nobody was out on the island. Usually I could expect to find at least Jack sitting by himself. But the island was as empty as my sister's head.

I went to Trevor's house and knocked on the door. When his mom opened up, she informed me that Trevor was busy reading.

I wasn't surprised that Trevor was reading. Even before my closet had begun spitting things out, Trevor had been into books. He bought books, borrowed books, and checked them out from the library. He was a member of a book club and an honorary member of a book society. It used to be a problem in our friendship, but now that I was beginning to see how interesting books could be, I didn't think Trevor was quite as geeky. So it wasn't surprising to find out that he was currently reading. What was surprising was what happened when I knocked on Teddy's door and his older brother with the gross mustache who always called me champ answered.

I got almost the same answer from Aaron's older sister, who also had sort of a gross mustache. She always called me Backside because my last name is Burnside.

Now here's where it gets even more eerie. When I went to Rourk's house, his mom answered the door and told me to come inside. She went down the hall to Rourk's room, and when she came back, she looked like she had seen a ghost.

When I got to Jack's house, he answered the door with a book in his hands. He didn't seem embarrassed or bothered.

I FELT LIKE DOING SOME READING.

REALLY? AND THAT'S THE BOOK YOU CHOSE?

IT CAN'T HURT MY CHANCES. BESIDES, IT'S A PRETTY SICK BOOK.

It was suddenly perfectly clear why all my friends were reading. They were looking to have a better shot at Kat liking them. I thought it was great that they were trying to improve their minds. I just wanted them to improve their minds at a better time.

I couldn't find Kat, and I had no idea where to look for her or why she was here. I had already finished *The Hunger Games* and was halfway through *Catching Fire*. Usually the old lab supplies in my closet dripped and mixed with a few books. But the mix wasn't obvious this time. The only thing I really had to go on was that she had called me Eric once. I didn't remember there being an Eric in *The Hunger Games*. I needed my friends' help, but they were all too busy reading. Weird.

I NEED TO FIND HER.

WELL, IF SHE'S ANYTHING LIKE THIS GIRL IN THE BOOK, SHE'S PROBABLY NOT EASY TO FIND.

When I got home I was in for a few more surprises. The table was set and my family was sitting down to dinner. That wasn't too surprising. What sort of caught me off guard was seeing Kat next to Libby.

I had a feeling that Kat bumping into my sister wasn't an accident. She probably stalked Libby just so she could get invited to dinner—which was kind of weird when you considered what had happened at dinner yesterday.

After a much cleaner dinner than last night, my mom decided to act fancy by serving ice cream out on the patio by the pool. We usually didn't have dessert, and we almost never ate outside, but the weather was good and we had a guest. Little did they know the guest had come from my closet, but if it meant getting ice cream, I was happy to keep my mouth shut.

My dad got out his guitar and sang while Libby and Kat braided each other's hair. To make things even more uncomfortable, Tuffin danced while my mom did some weird humming.

I think they were trying to show Kat what an American family does after dinner, but it looked like a lie. Typically things were more like this after dinner:

CHAPTER 13

THINGS MUST CHANGE

After the ice cream, my dad went inside to put his guitar away, and my mom went in to straighten up. Libby ran off to get a magazine that she wanted Kat to see. That left me alone with Kat and Tuffin.

WELL, THIS IS NICE.

Tuffin was done with his ice cream and began throwing it around so Puck could lick it up. It didn't bother me that much until Tuffin took a chunk and heaved it into the pool. Puck ran for it and jumped into the water.

Most dogs could swim, but not Puck. He was so fat that his little legs just spun him in circles. He had fallen in once before, and we had to snag him with the net and push him over to the pool steps. This time, before I could grab the net, Kat sprang up and jumped into the water. She moved so fast it was like a blur.

Kat grabbed hold of Puck and pushed him back to
the edge, where I reached down and pulled him out.

Tuffin hugged Puck while I went to help Kat out
of the pool. But suddenly she looked different—very
different!

I couldn't decide if I should pass out, flip out, or
get out.

Kat had gone all mermaid on me! Her bottom half was a giant fish tail, and her hair was now red. She had on a seashell bikini top over her jacket and white pearls around her neck. Plus, her left hand looked like a fin.

I FEEL DIFFERENT.

Kat gazed up at me, smiling. She didn't seem very surprised by her new shape. I, however, couldn't really speak.

I...YOU...WHAT?

I didn't know what to do. Kat couldn't get out of the pool now because she had no legs. I also had a strong feeling that she probably needed to stay in the water, being a mermaid and all. She swam across the pool and jumped up. Tuffin turned around and stared at her.

TUNA FISH!

I knew Libby would come back any second and I would have more explaining to do than I was capable of explaining. I had to get Kat out and away. I jumped into the pool and picked her up. She put her arms around my neck and her tail over my arm. I had never liked the smell of fresh fish, so it wasn't the greatest moment of my life.

I lifted Kat out of the pool and set her in the empty wheelbarrow that my mom used for hauling manure for the garden. I then pushed Kat as fast as I could to the back of our yard and out the gate into the alley.

There was a man named Dean who had a saltwater pool. He lived down the alley and he was an airline pilot. Because of that, everyone called him Pilot Dean. I don't even know what his real last name is. He was friends with my parents, and whenever he went out of town to fly a plane, he had me water his plants and take in his mail. I knew he wasn't home at the moment because my mom had me water his plants earlier today. I was thinking I could place Kat in his pool until I figured out what else do. Kat liked the idea, so I kept pushing.

When we reached the back gate of Pilot Dean's yard, I pulled open the latch and pushed the wheelbarrow in. The backyard was completely dark. There were no porch lights on and the windows of the house were dark.

I wheeled Kat to the edge of the pool, and as gently as I could I dumped her in. She went into the water with a small splash. I couldn't see anything, so I lay down on my stomach and whispered into the water.

Kat popped up just a few inches from my face. I could barely see her smile thanks to the black of night.

I had no idea what Kat was talking about. Leave it to a fish girl to bring up love at a time like this. All I knew was that in Pilot Dean's pool there was a mermaid who had originally come from my closet. I told Kat I'd be back, and she splashed her tail and swam to the other side. I ran home as fast as I could. When I got back, my mom and dad were coming out of the house with Libby. Tuffin was still having a fit.

WHERE'S OUR FOREIGN FRIEND? DID YOU SCARE HER OFF?

FISH, FIN, FIN!

Tuffin wouldn't stop saying *fin* and pointing to the pool. Luckily my dad thought he was just talking

about where Kat was from. Apparently, he had
forgotten that he thought she was from Panama.

I couldn't get Kat off my mind. I was confused,
bewildered, and concerned. My body was having a hard
time knowing how to act. I was worried and excited at
the same time.

I felt pretty certain that she would be okay in Pilot Dean's pool, but there was a real sense of urgency to figure out what I needed to do before anyone discovered her. I'm pretty sure the sight of a mermaid would be something that I wouldn't be able to explain.

I knew I needed to do some research, but I also knew that I couldn't do it until my family was asleep. So I yawned really loud and tried to drop a few hints about everyone going to bed.

Strangely, everyone seemed okay with my suggestion except Tuffin. He agreed to go to bed but only if he could sing us a song first. So we all stood around while he sang.

Everyone besides me thought his song was cute. Luckily nobody took it seriously. As soon as Tuffin was done singing, my mom took him inside and tucked him in while my dad gave Libby and me one last lesson.

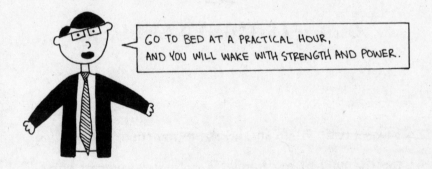

GO TO BED AT A PRACTICAL HOUR, AND YOU WILL WAKE WITH STRENGTH AND POWER.

I was planning to go to bed. I just wasn't planning to sleep.

CHAPTER 14

OLD-FASHIONED ANSWERS

I was tired, so staying awake in my room and waiting for the rest of my family to fall asleep wasn't easy. I slapped myself so many times I hardly recognized myself.

Eventually I could hear my dad snoring, and I felt pretty confident that everyone else was asleep. I opened my bedroom door and snuck quietly down the hall. I turned on our computer and looked up the book *The Little Mermaid*. I was surprised to find that it was a short story. I found a copy online and read it.

It didn't take me very long to read the whole thing, and let me say, it was not my favorite story. It was all about mermaids falling in love and wanting to be human. I needed to know more, so I turned

off the computer and went into the kitchen. On the
counter near the toaster, we had a small, portable
TV with a videotape player built into it.

It was really old, and my mom used it to play
videos for Tuffin. I guess in the olden days they used
to make movies on things called videotapes.

My family had a bunch of old videotapes, and Tuffin would shove them into the little TV and watch kid movies for hours.

I picked up the little TV and grabbed the video I was looking for, then I snuck back to my room without waking anyone up. I locked my door, plugged in the TV, and slipped in the movie.

I felt kind of weird watching one of Tuffin's movies, but I was hoping that I could discover something about Kat's purpose and story. I don't want to embarrass myself, but I was so busy watching the movie that I didn't notice I had a visitor.

Jack climbed into my window. It was late and he should have been at home sleeping, but he had been carving soap under the moonlight on the island and he saw my window glowing. I had no choice but to tell him everything. I told him about how Kat had fallen into the pool and had *become* Katfish. I told

him she was at Pilot Dean's and how it was important

that I watch *The Little Mermaid* to learn as much

as possible. I thought he was going to make fun of

me for the movie, but he just said,

I LOVE THE SONG
COMING UP.

It was kind of strange watching *The Little Mermaid*

with Jack in my dark room, but I'm pretty sure we had

done weirder things when we were younger.

I FOUND THIS
BOX OF ADULT
DIAPERS. WANNA
TRY 'EM?

I THINK
I'LL PASS.

When the movie ended, I wasn't sure if I had learned anything about Kat's purpose. I knew that she had called me Eric, which was the name of the guy the mermaid in the movie liked, but I wasn't sure how, or if, I could get Kat to have legs again.

Jack went home, and I changed into my pajamas. I then snuck out to the kitchen to put the TV back. Since I was already out there, I decided to make myself a midnight snack. For some reason, I was craving a certain something.

CHAPTER 15

RECKLESS DRIVER

Sunday was a mess. My family went to church in the morning. The air-conditioning wasn't working inside the chapel, and light coming through the stained-glass window was making us extra warm. Libby believed it was a sign of how the heavens thought she was beautiful. Tuffin felt differently. He was too hot, and he had gorged himself on scrambled eggs at home. So when the preacher wouldn't stop talking and our bench got super warm, Tuffin lost his breakfast all over Libby.

After we got home and Libby got cleaned up, more mess happened. Tim Knollmiller, one of the older neighborhood kids, crashed into our mailbox with his mom's station wagon. Tim had just gotten his license, and everyone knew he drove too fast. Now he claimed the mailbox had jumped out at him.

My dad was actually really nice to Tim. He told him a story about how he had accidentally knocked over a can of paint while painting a fence when he was a kid.

SO YOU CAN SEE, I'VE BEEN THERE.

I GUESS THAT'S THE SAME. CAN I PLEASE GO NOW?

There was no damage to Tim's mom's car and the mailbox was fixable, so my dad let Tim go but with a warning.

KEEP YOUR EYES ON THE ROAD AND YOU'LL GROW OLD.
IF YOUR EYES LOOK AWAY, YOU COULD BE DEAD TODAY.

Tim thanked him for the advice and drove off quickly. I helped my dad repair the mailbox, wanting all the while to get away and check on Kat. I didn't know exactly when Pilot Dean would be home, and I was worried about her. So once the mailbox was fixed, I made a couple of sandwiches and hiked down the alley and over to Pilot Dean's house. When I got there I could hear someone talking in the backyard. I opened the gate slowly, and there was Jack sitting on the edge of the pool, having a conversation with Kat. She was still very much a mermaid. Jack was wearing a nice shirt and had his hair combed back. He looked upset about something.

Jack stood up and noticed me for the first time. He seemed embarrassed to be there and kind of sad about something.

Jack walked off dejectedly. After the gate had closed, I kneeled down and offered Kat a sandwich. She ate it really fast. So I offered her another.

She finished the second one even quicker. I gave her both my sandwiches and the whole bag of potato chips. She was like a vacuum.

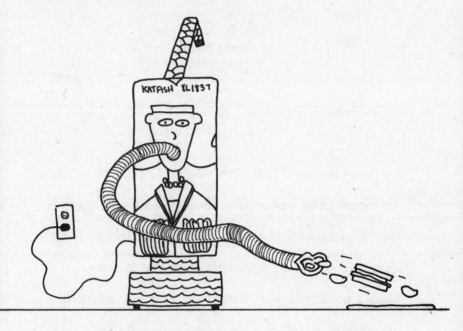

Kat started to go on and on about things she liked about me. Normally I would have killed for a girl to list things about me that were good, but I kind of felt like Kat wasn't talking to me exactly.

I was the one? The Little Mermaid part of Kat was concerning me. I needed to find out what was going on so that I could figure out what I was supposed to do. She had said she was here to help me and now I wasn't so sure. I just couldn't see how I could make a mermaid fit into my life. I had read *The Little Mermaid*, watched the movie, read *The Hunger Games*, watched the movie, and now I was reading *Catching Fire*. I had all the information, but I wasn't even sure how to move her around or where to put her. I told her I was worried about her condition, and she said,

I reminded her that she was supposed to be helping me smooth things over with Janae. She was all set to tell me about something when Mr. Foote's gong rang out two streets over. I was looking right at Kat, so I was pretty certain that she wasn't the one who gonged it.

I let her know she had already said that. Things were getting uncomfortable. Kat's personalities were much more distinct than the past creatures'. When she was speaking as a mermaid, her voice was soft and almost a whisper. But when the Katniss part came out, she was much *bolder*. Kat shook her head and the *bolder* part started talking.

LISTEN, ROB, IGNORE THE FISH PART OF ME. SHE'S BOY CRAZY. AND SHE REALLY WANTS TO SING.

WHY CAN'T SHE?

I WON'T LET HER, NOT YET. THE TIME'S NOT RIGHT, AND WE'VE GOT TO SOLVE YOUR PROBLEM.

I wanted to point out that she was a big part of my problem, but I didn't have the heart. I talked with Kat for about an hour. She wanted to know everything about me. I told her everything I could think of. I told her about Janae and how *badly* I had messed things up at my school. I also told her about the funstival and how Principal Smelt was putting on a Fun-ger Games contest.

SO HE LIKES PUNS?

YEP.

PUN PEOPLE WORRY ME.

I told Kat about how I was going to play in the band for the funstival. She jumped out of the water as I stood up. I also told her how I had read and watched *The Little Mermaid*. The fish part of her liked that.

Her Katniss part apologized. We talked some more, and she told me about herself. I really liked Kat, but I could see now that I didn't like her the way I liked Janae. It was cool to have a friend who was a girl. Oh yeah—and a fish. Kat confessed to me that part of her was really hungry and another part of her just wanted to sing. I told her I needed to get home but that I would bring her food every three hours. She said she would miss me, but she was more worried about the sandwiches.

I ran home and made six more sandwiches. I dropped them back off with Kat and then jogged to Trevor's house. He was waiting outside with his guiro.

LET'S DO THIS!

Principal Smelt and his group, Leftover Angst, always practiced on Sunday afternoons in Principal Smelt's open garage. He and the other band member would play music for anyone who wanted to stop by and listen. Not many people did. When we got to the garage they were already practicing. The other member was Mr. Pickel. Everyone called him Pickle. He taught Italian to the gifted students of Softrock Middle School. I hadn't even spoken to him *before,* and now that we were in the group, he still *didn't* speak. Principal Smelt did all the talking.

The things we sang didn't *seem* very cultured— they *seemed* dumb.

I just kept hitting my piece of wood while Trevor slid his stick up and down the guiro. It sounded horrible, but Principal Smelt felt differently.

After practice I went with Trevor to the mall because he needed to look for a costume to wear to the funstival. I didn't mind shopping with Trevor, but he was too obsessed with his guiro. He couldn't put the thing away.

We left the mall as soon as Trevor found a costume. He then went to his house to practice, and I headed home to make some more sandwiches. I had been making so much food that we were running out of normal ingredients, so I had to use what I could find.

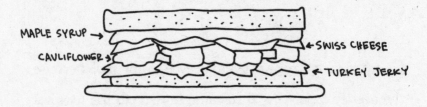

MAPLE SYRUP →
CAULIFLOWER →
← SWISS CHEESE
← TURKEY JERKY

It wasn't something that I would enjoy, but I had a feeling Kat would eat every bite.

CHAPTER 16

WATER BABIES

Monday morning I got up early so that I could get ready and slip out to school before anyone woke up. I took a shower, and after getting dressed, I found Tuffin in the kitchen, washing his feet in the sink.

I think he was trying to make his legs turn into a fish tail. He had talked nonstop about Kat having a fin, but luckily nobody took him seriously. I left a sticky note on the fridge for my mom and headed out.

I WENT TO
SCHOOL EARLY.
I JUST CAN'T
WAIT TO LEARN!

I ran down the alley to deliver the sandwiches to Kat. Kat saw me and quickly swam up to the side of the pool. She shook her head, jumped out of the water, and began to give me a hard time.

HOW DARE YOU STAY AWAY, ERIC?

IS THE HUNGER PART OF YOU AROUND?

I gave Kat all the food I had brought and told her I would be back after school to feed her more. She surprised me by leaping up and grabbing my shirt. She pulled me into the water and dragged me across the pool to the other side near the fountain as I choked and sputtered. It all happened so fast I could barely breathe. I had no idea why she had pulled me in, but as we surfaced next to some pool floaties, Kat whispered,

I could hear Pilot Dean coming out the back door of his house. He was home and looking to have an early morning swim. He was also in for a big surprise.

We ducked down as low as we could. He stopped
near the edge of the pool and took off his shirt.

It was uncomfortable enough to see Pilot Dean
without a shirt, but it got even worse when he
started to do some preswim stretches.

The pool floaties were hiding us okay, but if Pilot Dean jumped in, we would be spotted for sure. He kept stretching and making odd noises. Then he put on his goggles and turned to the pool. As he leaped into the air, Kat wrapped her arms around me and shot up out of the water to the edge of the pool.

Her timing was perfect. Pilot Dean didn't see us because he was jumping in. We quickly made ourselves look like statues next to his fountains.

Pilot Dean just kept swimming laps. After what seemed like his hundredth lap, I realized that I had to do something to get out of this. I couldn't put Kat back into the pool. I also couldn't bring her to my house. She needed water, and I needed to get to school or I'd be in a whole new kind of trouble. I couldn't think of what to do. My mind began to sizzle under the pressure.

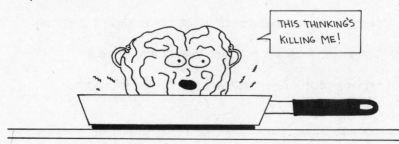

THIS THINKING'S KILLING ME!

I had an idea. I suddenly remembered something at my school that I might be able to hide Kat in. It wasn't the greatest plan, but it was all I could come up with.

As Pilot Dean was swimming the other way, I picked up Kat and carried her to the wheelbarrow that was still sitting by the back gate. We then dashed out the gate and into the alley without him spotting us. I ran as fast as I could, knowing that Kat needed water, and also knowing that I needed to get to Softrock Middle School before all the students began showing up.

I got to school in good time and put Kat in the safe place I had thought of. I knew she couldn't stay there forever, but it was okay for now. My clothes were still wet from the pool, and my arms and face were covered in sweat from the running. I bumped into Janae as I was wheeling the empty wheelbarrow out the door. For the first time in a while she actually spoke to me. I kind of wish she hadn't.

I hid the wheelbarrow behind the school sign and then went to the bathroom to try to clean myself up. As I was drying myself, Mark Delgado came in.

Mark Delgado was probably the coolest kid at school. He had a mustache and chest hair. Everyone called him Got-to-Go because whenever he left a room he would click his fingers and say,

For some reason girls thought it was cool and other boys thought it was funny. Everyone besides me wanted to hang around Mark. Principal Smelt had even picked him to be the master of ceremonies at the funstival

tonight. Still, I didn't really like him. Mostly because when we were younger and on the same baseball team, he had told me that if I wet my pants while I was at bat the umpire had to let me go to first base. I don't know why I believed him, but for some reason I tried it.

Even worse, the umpire didn't let me go to first. I had tried not to talk to Mark since then. Now, as he strutted into the bathroom with his mustache and chest hairs, I was drying my armpits with toilet paper.

Mark Delgado is not one of my favorite people.

CHAPTER 17

WHY ME?

The rest of the school day wasn't quite so wet. It was crazy how amped up everyone was. People were talking loud and acting like school wasn't so bad. Each classroom was excitedly setting up for the Fun-ger Games Funstival tonight. The halls were decorated with banners everywhere.

1ST ANNUAL

FUN-GER GAMES FUNSTIVAL

A FESTIVAL OF FUN

WEAR A COSTUME — VOTE FOR YOUR FAVORITE CLASSROOM

I checked on Kat twice, and she was doing okay. If I could get her out of her hiding place after school, everything would be all right. Principal Smelt was running around happily checking the rooms and making sure everyone was ready to have a blast tonight.

YOU READY TO HAVE A BLAST?

I GUESS.

YOU GUESS RIGHT!

The plan for his Fun-ger Games was that twelve different classrooms would compete. Each of the twelve rooms had been decorated, and tonight when the parents and families came they would vote for their favorite. The classroom with the lowest vote would be eliminated first. Then the next classroom and the next until there was just one classroom standing. The winning classroom would receive a blueberry pie for each student.

GET IT? LIKE IN THE BOOK.

IN THE BOOK THEY WEREN'T BLUEBERRIES. THEY WERE NIGHTLOCK. AND THEY WERE POISONOUS.

WELL, WE'LL JUST HAVE TO MAKE DO WITH WHAT WE HAVE.

My homeroom class did a pretty good job decorating. We had chosen to make our room all about sponsors. In *The Hunger Games* there were sponsors who helped the kids stay alive. So we had drawn posters of different companies and sponsors. In the end, our room looked like a giant ad for everything.

When the last bell rang I ran from class to where I had hidden Kat. I knew that if she stayed where she was she would be found during the funstival. As I was racing I turned a corner and ran right into Principal Smelt. I tried to get away from him, but he put his arm around my shoulder and started leading me down the hall for what he was calling a last-minute . . .

It was horrible. No matter how much I begged and pleaded, Principal Smelt would not let me get out of practicing. To make matters worse, he made us practice for almost two hours. As we were practicing, other teachers and students began to set up the gym for the funstival. They put all the booths up and lined the refreshments on tables. I was feeling worried about Kat, and I felt even worse when I saw one of the school's janitors wheeling in her hiding place.

He set the dunk tank on the far end of the gym near the doors. If the janitor took off the cover he would see

Kat and then everything would be over. Someone would capture her and take her away for scientific purposes, and I would be in trouble, trouble, trouble . . .

... WITH A CAPITAL T. WHICH RHYMES WITH D. WHICH STANDS FOR DOOMED!

Nobody had any idea what my life was like these days. Most middle school students had enough to worry about without adding crazy creatures to the mix. I know my closet was trying to point out that books are a part of my life whether I like it or not. There were lessons I had learned and things about my life that were now more interesting due to the books that I had read, but the truth of the matter was that I just wanted things to smooth out for a while. I wanted my school to not hate me and for Janae to like me. I think that Beardy and my closet had the wrong definition of help. Kat had been up-front with me, telling me that she was here to make things better, but at the moment things felt way worse. Kat was about to be discovered, and I was in for a whole new level of mess.

At five o'clock Principal Smelt made everyone exit the gymnasium. He locked the doors and sent us all home to . . .

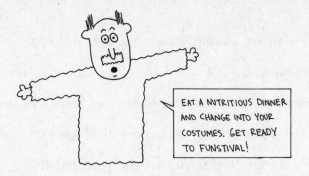

Kat was now locked in the gym. I tried to get
back in, but it was no use. I explained the situation
to Trevor. He was too excited about the funstival
and the horrible music we were going to be a part
of to worry about Kat. I couldn't get him to focus on
my situation.

CHAPTER 18

~

FIRST ANNUAL FUN-GER GAMES FUNSTIVAL

When I got home I changed into some clothes that kind of looked like a costume and then I joined my family for dinner.

It was bad enough that I had to play in Principal Smelt's awful band, but it was even worse that most of my family would be there to see it.

After dinner we piled into the car and drove to Softrock Middle School. When we got there the parking lot was already packed. I could see that the people from P.E.E.T.A. had set up a booth across from the school and were protesting against students reading a book that they had not approved.

The parents' association hadn't read *The Hunger Games* yet, so they weren't sure the students of

Softrock Middle School should be having a funstival about it.

They yelled a few things at us as we parked and went inside.

We moved away quickly, mainly because they were spitting a lot as they talked. When we got inside the school, everybody was dressed up in costumes. We were all handed little round disks labeled...

It was a play on the Hunger Games author's name. I'm not sure why Principal Smelt's face was on it. The idea was that people had fifteen minutes to

vote for the decorations they liked *best* by putting
the coins in special bowls in each classroom. The
room with the most votes would win. I put my coin
in my pocket as my mom was telling us all to . . .

STAY TOGETHER!

At that, my dad took Tuffin to vote for the
classroom they liked best and I took off to find Kat.
I was worried that someone had already found her
in the dunk tank. If any adults saw her they would *be*
screaming and shouting to the world that mermaids
were real. I had listened to the car radio on the way
over trying to hear any news about a mermaid spotting
or information on how much trouble I would *be* in.

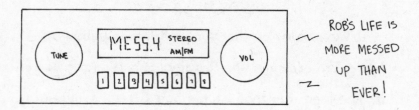

ROB'S LIFE IS
MORE MESSED
UP THAN
EVER!

Luckily, I didn't hear anything about me. The halls of the school were packed. People were hurrying to put their Suzanne Coins in the boxes to cast their votes before time ran out. I voted for my classroom and then made my way to the gymnasium. When I walked in I couldn't believe my eyes.

The dunk tank was uncovered, and Kat was sitting up on the seat, smiling. There was a line of people waiting to throw baseballs at her as she swished her tail in the water.

I don't know why I hadn't thought about it, but since so many people were in costumes Kat just fit right in.

I worked my way behind the dunk tank. I stuck

my face up and spoke to her over the back of

the booth.

Kat insisted I go. I walked away, wondering what to do. Trevor spotted me, and I walked over to him.

A bell rang, and Principal Smelt came over to the loudspeaker. He cleared his throat and announced,

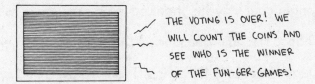

Everyone clapped. The gymnasium was loud and exciting and warm due to all the people coming in. There was a little stage set up on the side and booths where people were buying tickets to play games. It would have been pretty fun-ger if I hadn't

been so nervous about Kat and having to play in the band. After about fifteen minutes Mark Delgado stepped onto the stage and tapped the microphone to test it. Everyone started to quiet down and pay attention. Mark welcomed the crowd to the . . .

...FIRST ANNUAL FUN-GER GAMES! MAY THE ODDS BE EVER IN YOUR FAVOR. OF COURSE THAT WON'T BE HARD SEEING HOW WE ALL GO TO SOFTROCK MIDDLE SCHOOL.

Everyone laughed at his dumb joke. Then in his annoyingly cool way he thanked everyone for coming and voting. He also announced that Principal Smelt had begun counting the coins. I looked over and saw Principal Smelt sitting at a table near the edge of the gymnasium.

... SIX PLUS ONE EQUALS SEVEN. SEVEN PLUS ONE EQUALS EIGHT. EIGHT PLUS...

MRS. HYDEN-FINCH

MR. DUNNELL

LEFTOVER ANGST

MS. JENKINS

MRS. MANGES

MR. PETE

The crowd watched him count. When he was done he handed the results to Mark Delgado.

THE RESULTS ARE IN. I WILL NOW READ OFF THE TWO CLASSROOMS WITH THE LOWEST VOTES.

Then like in *The Hunger Games*, the eliminated classrooms were projected on the wall while Mark made a cannon noise.

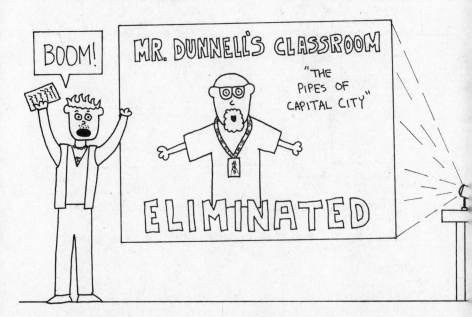

BOOM!

MR. DUNNELL'S CLASSROOM

"THE PIPES OF CAPITAL CITY"

ELIMINATED

After the first two classrooms were eliminated,
Mark promised more results in a minute, and everyone clapped. I could see my dad walking around in the
crowd with Tuffin up on his shoulders. The two of them
were looking at the athletic equipment we had in the
gym. My dad's company had sold most of the
equipment to our school.

Every five minutes Mark Delgado would loudly
announce the two classrooms with the next lowest
votes.

It was kind of startling to hear Mark yell "Boom" every five minutes. Everyone would jump and clap. The gym became more and more packed as people continued to pour in and classrooms were eliminated. When it came down to only two classrooms, Mark Delgado turned the microphone over to Principal Smelt to announce the winning room. The crowd quieted as Principal Smelt spoke.

Mrs. Hyden-Finch's class won the contest with their zombie-themed room. It had nothing to do with the Hunger Games, but I guess people loved it.

After Mrs. Hyden-Finch's class came up and got their *blueberry pies* Principal Smelt announced,

NOW FOR SOMETHING EVEN MORE EXCITING! NOT ONLY IS MY BAND PLAYING, BUT WE HAVE TWO VERY SPECIAL GUESTS!

He told the crowd that Trevor was playing *because* of his guiro skills. He then said that I was playing because . . .

I had really hurt my school when Pinocula was here, and I was about to pay for it. Our first song went pretty well. I thought that Trevor was a little heavy on the guiro, but the crowd seemed to like it. Usually when Principal Smelt played, everyone tried to get away, but tonight it seemed like the whole town of Temon was here and actually enjoying the show. As I was tearing it up on the wood block, I noticed that Mark Delgado was talking to Kat across the room.

I don't think I'm jealous—I'm just nervous. For
some reason the sight of Kat talking to Mark
seemed like a bad idea. I could see Mark laughing
over something Kat said. I didn't know what they
were talking about, but I knew it probably wouldn't
be good for me.

CHAPTER 19

BLACKED OUT

I played my wood block and Trevor played the guiro pretty well. It was actually fun, but I was still uneasy about what Kat had said to Mark. When our third song ended, the crowd cheered like we had done something good. We all took a bow.

Before we could set down our instruments and the funstival officially ended, Mark stepped up to the microphone to make a surprise announcement. Everyone leaned forward as if what was about to be announced was going to change the world. Even I was excited until Mark said,

AS YOU ALL KNOW, A FEW WEEKS AGO ROB BURNSIDE LET US DOWN. NOW I'VE BEEN TOLD THAT IN AN EFFORT TO MAKE THINGS RIGHT HE HAS A SPECIAL SONG HE'D LIKE TO SING.

Mark didn't need to remind the school. They all knew I had lied to them and ruined our dance. But not only had Mark reminded them, he was now talking about me singing. I couldn't believe it. I could hear the words he was saying, but they were so shocking my ears were having a fit.

UH-UH, NO WAY!

I'LL HAVE NO PART OF THIS!

I couldn't sing. I could barely whistle. I knew that somehow Kat was involved in this. She and Mark had been talking, and this was the result. Well, there was no way I was going to sing. I didn't even know any songs. I looked at Principal Smelt, hoping he would clear things up. Apparently, that wasn't the plan.

Principal Smelt and Mr. Pickel pushed me into the light of the single spotlight shining down. Trevor lifted his guiro as if to salute and cheer me on. The gymnasium was dark, but I could still make out the crowd staring me down.

I couldn't *believe* this was happening! I had nothing to sing. The room went completely quiet. Even the really little kids shut up to give me the *best possible* chance to embarrass myself.

SHHH. LET'S WATCH THIS KID MAKE A FOOL OF HIMSELF.

MY DAD'S A NERD

I cleared my throat and scanned the crowd, trying to think of what to say. I wanted everyone to know that I was sorry, but there was no way I was going to sing about it. I felt like Katniss in *The Hunger Games* as she was forced to be the tribute and play the game. The biggest difference is that she was brave and capable and probably could sing if she had needed to. As I was looking out, I noticed that in the dark, back behind the crowd, Kat was pulling herself up and leaning over the side of the dunk tank. She snatched a bow and arrow off the back of some kid dressed as Robin Hood.

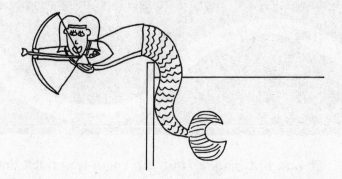

Then she let the arrow fly. I just stood there with my mouth open as it sailed over my head.

The arrow flew across the room and hit the switch to the spotlight. The light went out, making the gymnasium completely dark. Before anyone could react, a beautiful voice filled the air.

THERE IS A LOVELY SONG IN ME, LIKE A SMALL CHILD WHO WANTS TO BE FREE. I ONLY WANT TO BE HEARD.

It was Kat singing, but the room was dark and the acoustics were making it difficult to tell exactly where the singing was coming from. Before the lights went out, I had been standing there looking like I was about to sing, so I had a bad feeling that everyone thought it was me.

AND NOW THAT I'VE FOUND MY VOICE I HOPE TO SING MY SONG. I WANT THE WORLD TO KNOW I LOVE THEM.

I don't know what the song was that Kat was singing, but the words were horrible. Her voice was really beautiful. In the dark I could see how someone might think it was a really lovely boy's voice. I just stood there wondering if I should scream out to let people know it wasn't me. I threw my hands up to holler, but as the verse ended and I was standing there with my mouth hanging open, someone turned the lights back on.

Kat had stopped singing. The crowd was completely quiet. I could see Janae. I was so embarrased. I knew that I would now probably need to move to some glass bubble at the bottom of the sea to get away from everyone.

The silence ended as everyone in the crowd began

to laugh. Principal Smelt slapped me on the back.

People thought what I had done was funny. They had no idea that Kat's heartfelt song was anything other than me trying to make them laugh.

People kept slapping me on the back and telling me how clever and funny I was.

I tried my hardest to act like I had been in on the joke, but I was more concerned about Kat. She wasn't in the dunk tank any longer, and I knew that she needed water. I got Trevor, and we pushed through the crowd to find Kat. She wasn't behind any of the other booths or displays.

CHAPTER 20

BAFFLING

Trevor and I split up to see if we could find Kat
faster that way. As I was running behind the school,
dodging families and students heading to their cars,
I saw Janae. She was walking by herself, and she
didn't look as mad at me as she had in the past.

I was surprised she was even talking to me. I expected her to either ignore me or yell. I had hurt her feelings, and to make things even more awkward, I had just sung in front of the whole community.

I couldn't remember what I had sung. I knew the words were kind of dumb, but I couldn't remember what the message was. But Janae was smiling at me and she had said she liked it, so I went with it.

Janae handed me one of the small pieces of white paper we had cut up and put into those balloons a few days ago.

ROB ᴵ ᴼᵈᶜˢ LIKES ᵘ˗ ᵉ YOU ᵉ

The water had smudged it in my favor this time. What Jack had written was "Rob never likes making you mad," but it had gotten smeared just perfectly. I looked at Janae.

I'M REALLY SORRY ABOUT EVERYTHING I DID TO YOU.

For the record, I want to let you know that apologizing is pretty cool. I mean, most of the time saying you're sorry is kind of painful. Apologizing to

Janae was different. Janae leaned in and kissed me. I'd draw a picture of it, but the moment seemed a little

I dropped my wood block, and it knocked against the ground. Janae stepped back and smiled at me. I returned the smile as she walked away, leaving me to wonder about what just happened.

My confused thoughts were interrupted by the sound of a car horn. I looked up to see Trevor hanging out

the front seat window of Tim Knollmiller's mom's
station wagon.

I ran up to the car and hopped into the back seat.
Kat was sitting there, looking happy to see me. She
was smiling as if she knew she had accomplished
what she needed to.

Trevor had found Kat hiding in the school's fountain out front. She had dragged herself there, looking for water. After Trevor found Kat he spotted Tim and talked him into giving us a ride to my house. Like everyone else, Tim thought Kat was wearing a costume. Tim was also happy to give us a ride.

I FIGURE I OWE YOU SINCE I WRECKED YOUR MAILBOX. LISTEN, SINCE I DON'T HAVE ANY PLANS TONIGHT, YOU GUYS WANNA HANG? I THINK MY MOM WENT GROCERY SHOPPING TODAY. SHE GETS SOME PRETTY GOOD STUFF. THERE COULD EVEN BE FRUIT ROLL-UPS.

Before I could explain to Tim why we didn't want to hang out with him or eat any of his family's groceries, Kat spoke up.

WE CAN'T. WE HAVE TO GET BACK HOME.

I figured I would get Kat home and then decide what to do after that. Tim pulled out of the parking lot and drove quickly down the street to my house. I was happy Tim knew how to go fast. It was pretty important that we beat my parents home. When we got to my house I was relieved to see that my family hadn't beat us. Trevor and I got Kat out of the car and thanked Tim.

YOU SURE YOU DON'T WANT TO COME OVER? MY MOM MIGHT HAVE GOTTEN STRING CHEESE.

We said no three times and Tim left. We then carried Kat through the front door. I was going to take her to the swimming pool, but she had other plans.

Kat insisted, so we carried her down the hall. Before we could get there, we ran into one more obstacle.

The house was dark, and I had forgotten that Libby was home. She was wearing her ratty robe with her hair up and some sort of green mud on her face. Her eyes were covered with cucumber slices, so she couldn't see that I was holding a mermaid. We pushed past Libby, and she yelled at me,

I SHOULD HAVE BEEN AN ONLY CHILD.

We got to my room and shut the door. I turned on my bedroom light.

WHAT A SEA WITCH!

YEAH, TELL ME ABOUT IT.

Libby had looked a lot like the sea witch in *The Little Mermaid* movie. I would have to remember that insult. Trevor and I set Kat on my bed. She was smiling, but I could tell that she needed water and needed it soon.

Kat looked toward my closet and smiled. At that same moment, Beardy clicked and the closet door opened an inch.

I was hoping Wonk or Hairy might pop out again. I wouldn't have minded seeing Pinocula, but nothing came out. I realized what was about to happen and looked Kat in the eyes.

YOU'RE GOING IN?

I'M SORRY, BUT IT'S GOOD-BYE FOR NOW.

I couldn't think of what to say. I knew Kat couldn't stay forever. I also knew that I had probably reached the limit of where I could hide her. Of all the creatures from my closet, Kat had been the most honest and straightforward. She'd come to help me, and judging by the kiss Janae had given me earlier and everybody at school being nice again, I think she had succeeded.

IT'S BEEN WEIRD.

IT'LL PROBABLY BE WEIRDER.

WHAT'S THAT SUPPOSED TO MEAN?

Kat didn't answer. She nodded toward my dresser.
There, on top, were the items Wonk and Hairy had
left me. Next to those items were Kat's bow and
arrows. She had instructed Jack to put them there
after ringing the gong. Trevor was a little hurt that
Kat wasn't giving anything to him, so she quickly made
something up.

OH YEAH, FOR YOU
I GIVE WISDOM.

WOW, THAT'S
INVALUABLE.

Kat then leaned in and gave Trevor a kiss on the
cheek. That made him say "Wow" even louder.

WOW! I'M NEVER
WASHING AGAIN.

I helped Kat over to the closet. Before reaching for Beardy, she turned and gave me a hug. I don't want to be obnoxious or anything. I mean, my parents have always taught me to be humble, but I was really hitting it off with the ladies tonight.

Kat grabbed Beardy and pulled the door open a bit more. She then hopped a few inches behind the door and looked back at me.

Kat smiled. She hopped a few more inches and then disappeared into the closet. A giant wave followed.

Everything in my room was soaked. Beardy shut the door behind her and stared straight ahead like he usually did. I could tell from his expression that he had locked things up tight.

Trevor left through my window, and my parents came home a few minutes later. My dad stuck his head into my bedroom and congratulated me on my singing.

YOU SOUNDED LIKE A MANLY ANGEL.

THANKS, DAD.

It was hard for me to fall asleep. Kat had come quickly and changed things for the better. I guess I'm not really sure what I should write down here. I know that it's important for me to be keeping track of these things, but as weird as my closet was, it was finally beginning to feel pretty normal.

MY NAME IS ROBERT COLUMBO BURNSIDE AND I HAVE A CLOSET.

I read *Catching Fire* for half an hour and then I did what I knew must be done. I grabbed everything off my dresser, climbed out my window, and snuck down the street to Mr. Foote's yard. I wasn't as good with the bow and arrow as Kat was. On my third try I hit the gong.

ANOTHER ONE DOWN.

After ringing the gong I ran home and put the items back on my dresser before crawling into bed. I was actually pretty happy. I was happy to know that things might be smoother at school. I was happy that Janae and I were on good terms. And I was happy that all closets were not created equal. My happiness helped me sleep well. It's almost as if I had nothing to worry about. Of course, maybe I should have looked under my bed.

GOFISH

OBERT SKYE

If you heard a strange rattling sound in your closet and discovered a mythical creature there, what's the first thing you would do?
Duck behind my bed and scream. Actually, I'd probably scream and then duck.

Who is your favorite fictional character and why?
Willy Wonka. I like how odd he is and that he owns a chocolate factory. My goal is to have my own chocolate factory someday. I want to be like Willy.

Who or what did you most like to doodle when you were young?
I liked to doodle everything. Weird animals were my favorite subjects. I did a comic strip for my school called *Prep-punker*. It was about a goofy, preppy punk rocker. It was kind of my beginning in telling stories with pictures.

What sort of books did you enjoy most when you were young?
I loved anything funny and exciting. Those were my two favorite types of books to read then and now. I loved when a book made me laugh and caused my heart to beat fast. I always try to make my books have a lot of humor and exciting things happening in them.

If you could be any of the creatures from Rob's closet, which would you be and why?

It changes day to day. I would love to be Potterwookiee because I like both wands and Wookiees. I'd also like to be Batneezer. There is power in being created from a combination of LEGO and bat.

What problem would you want a mythical creature to help you solve?

Visibility. I've always wanted to be invisible. I'd like to sit on the top of a tall building without anyone seeing me. I could overlook the city in complete solitude and point at things that need to be pointed at.

If you were a character in any book, which book would you choose?

I'd be Rob from the Creature from My Closet series. He messes up a lot, but his life is hilarious—and a hilarious life is a life well lived.

Did you read comics as a kid? Do you have a favorite comic book character?

I read tons of comics and still do. I've always been a big Spider-Man fan. I also liked a lesser-known character named Captain Carrot. He was the leader of this amazing Zoo Crew.

What is your favorite movie of all time?

Return of the Jedi.

Can you tell us a little about your new series, *Geeked Out*?

This is such a fun series to write. It is the end of the world, but characters still have to get to class on time. Society needs a few heroes, and in this book they come from the most unlikely places. I'm super Geeked Out about it.

When Rob's family wins a trip to Colorado, something extra makes it into his luggage. Part Gollum, part Cat in the Hat, this is a creature unlike any other. . . .

THE CREATURE FROM MY CLOSET

THE LORD OF THE HAT

OBERT SKYE

Rob Burnside's troubles keep on coming in

THE LORD OF THE HAT!

BUMPS IN THE NIGHT

I didn't sleep well. It was cold and Jack snores—a
lot. I also kept hearing things. I wanted to wake my
friends up and go into the RV, but I knew they
would make fun of me for years. So I slept poorly,
and when I woke up, the first thing I said was,

I was uneasy. There was something going on, and I couldn't quite put my finger on it. My rhyming was not normal. The ULT I saw on the film was unusual. I knew that something was happening, but how could Beardy and my closet be messing with me so far from home? It wasn't like they could just phone it in.

After breakfast we drove for two hours and stopped at the world's biggest toothpick to take a picture.

We then drove another three hours and had a lunch of fried chicken near the world's largest collection of dice.

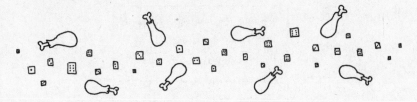

Then we drove about three more hours and reached our destination for the night in the town of Simmering, New Mexico. We stopped at another RV park near a drive-in movie theater that was no longer in operation.

We had dinner around another campfire, and my dad filled us in on what would be happening tomorrow.

WE WILL BE TAKING THE TRAIN TOMORROW MORNING. IT'S A FIVE-HOUR RIDE UP TO THE TOP OF THE MOUNTAINS, WHERE WE WILL BE STAYING IN ONE OF AMERICA'S OLDEST HOTELS.

GROSS.

My dad said that it was also one of the grandest. We would be in the town of Tolk for two nights. There would be horseback riding and tennis and hiking.

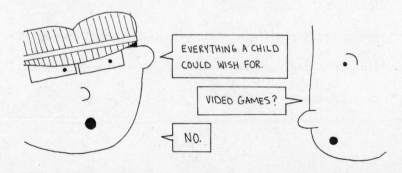

EVERYTHING A CHILD COULD WISH FOR.

VIDEO GAMES?

NO.

He then added that on the second night he would
be honored with an award for the outstanding small
business by the governor of New Mexico. This was
a family vacation, yes—but this was really about my
dad getting his award, and if we wanted to have any
fun we couldn't ruin this for him. So I said,

When everyone was done eating, my dad
suggested that we all hike over to the abandoned
drive-in theater and see if there were any ghosts. I
loved abandoned buildings. My grandpa once gave
me a book that was filled with pictures of buildings
that had been abandoned. They were all interesting
and creepy-looking. Now I would get to explore an

old drive-in. I was okay with that. So after dinner we cleaned up and walked as a group out of the RV park, across a road, and up to the drive-in. It was kind of a scary night, and Libby and Melany were acting more frightened than Tuffin. At the drive-in there was a rope holding an old gate closed. My dad pulled the rope, and the gate opened. We walked in to where cars used to park to watch movies. I could see the weathered old screen in the distance. Trevor started to panic.

I suggested we all run back to the RV and get the camera together, but my dad seemed to think it would be fine for me and Trevor to go alone. Tuffin wouldn't let Jack come, so it was just us two. We crossed the road and worked our way through the RV park. When we got to our RV, I heard something moving around inside. Trevor was about to blow the emergency safety whistle he was wearing when I said,

WAIT, LOOK!

I pointed toward the RV. There was a light on inside, and we could see the silhouette of something. Trevor adjusted his glasses.

WHAT'S THAT?

SOME SORT OF ANIMAL.

BUT IT'S WEARING A HAT.

THEY MAKE CLOTHES FOR ANIMALS THESE DAYS.

THAT'S NOT A NORMAL ANIMAL.

Trevor really wanted to blow his safety whistle, but I wouldn't let him. I had a pretty good idea of what we were looking at. I didn't think it was an accident that we ended up with nothing but Lord of the Rings books and Dr. Seuss stuff. I also thought there was a reason why I was rhyming so much lately. I told Trevor that I thought it was possible that Beardy had set something free from my closet and it had traveled with us here. I also told him that if I had to guess, I thought it might be part Dr. Seuss, part Lord of the Rings.

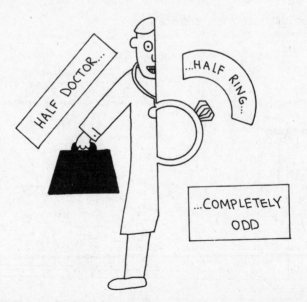

Trevor no longer wanted to blow his whistle. He wanted to open the RV door and get a look. Trevor loved the Lord of the Rings books. He had read them a couple of times. He also loved Dr. Seuss.

We could hear something knocking things over in the RV. We could also hear it saying,

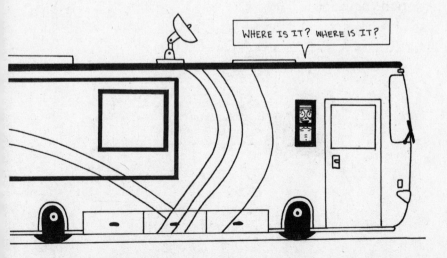

I wished my dad was there, but I knew that I couldn't go get him, because if the creature was from my closet, it would probably be best that my parents didn't know. They had no clue what my closet could do, and they'd be blue if they ever knew.

SORRY ABOUT THAT LAST LINE.
IT WASN'T SUPPOSED TO RHYME.

I opened the RV door and looked inside. There was a dish on the floor, and one of the cabinets was hanging open.

GO IN.

I WILL. GIVE ME A SECOND.

ONE-ONE-THOUSAND, TWO-ONE-THOUSAND. THAT'S TWO SECONDS—NOW GO!

This is a good example of how different my life had become. In the past I never would have gone into an RV with something strange knocking about in it. Now it was almost normal to be surrounded by strange.

I stepped into the RV and looked around. One light was on, but there were shadows everywhere. Trevor stepped in behind me. He had his hands and arms up over his face for protection.

TELL THEM WE MEAN NO HARM.

YOU TELL THEM.

Before either one of us could tell anyone
anything, something popped out of a cabinet and
flew toward us.

WHAT CREATURE WILL
COME OUT OF ROB'S CLOSET NEXT?

Look out for Obert Skye's
HILARIOUS NEW SERIES!

OBERT SKYE

GEEKED OUT

A LAME NEW WORLD

Society has fallen apart. Waddle Jr. High has become a dystopian outpost with divided cliques—Sox, Jocks, Goths, Loners, Freaks, Pens, Staffers, and yes, Geeks! Enter geeky Tip and all his highly original friends: brainy members of the AV club who decide it's their time to take charge. Together, they form a secret vigilante group: the League of Average and Mediocre Entities, better known as LAME. With everything going on in the world, their school could use a few heroes. What if those heroes have superpowers? Well, weird superpowers. Get ready. Better yet, get LAME.